Susan Yawn Tanner

Callahan in Action

Secret Staircase Books

Cat Callahan Mysteries
by Rebecca Barrett and Susan Yawn Tanner

Callahan on the Case
Callahan and the Horses of Hope
Callahan's Savannah Caper
Callahan Goes Rodeo
Callahan and the Spy
Callahan in Action
Callahan's Christmas Feast (short story)
A Callahan Christmas (short story)

Susan Yawn Tanner

Callahan in Action

Cat Callahan Mysteries, Book 6

Callahan in Action
Published by Secret Staircase Books, an imprint of
Columbine Publishing Group LLC
PO Box 416, Angel Fire, NM 87710

Book layout and design by Secret Staircase Books
Illustrations by Becky's Graphic Design, Jason Mark Schulz, Ken
Backer, Alancotton, Svetlana Dubovetcaia, Kalinin Dmitrii

First e-book edition: August, 2024
First paperback edition: August, 2024

An earlier version of this story was published in 2019 as *Trouble in Action*

Publisher's Cataloging-in-Publication Data

Tanner, Susan Yawn
Callahan in Action / by Susan Yawn Tanner.
p. cm.
ISBN 978-1649141811 (paperback)
ISBN 978-1649141828 (e-book)

1. Cat Callahan (Fictitious character)—Fiction. 2. Southern
Mysteries—Fiction. 3. Amateur sleuths—Fiction. I. Title

Cat Callahan Mystery Series, Book 6.
Tanner, Susan Yawn, Cat Callahan Mysteries.

BISAC : FICTION / Mystery.

813/.54

To Robert and Evelyn Dudley whose front yard my sister, brother, and I crossed every morning to catch the bus. Theirs was the first number we called when an animal was sick or injured. Whether domestic or wild, they cared for them all, nursing them to health if they could and consoling us if they couldn't. They were the neighbors you rarely find anymore, a fading breed filled with kindness and generosity.

Acknowledgements
Family makes us crazy or keeps us sane. My sister is my prayer warrior and sounding board. My brother is the ever-calm voice of sanity and reason.
I'm grateful for both.
Also, for those who help to polish my work before it's published, a special heartfelt thank you to my beta readers: Marcia Koopmann, Susan Gross, Sandra Anderson, Paula Webb, Isobel Tamney, Amy Connolley, Georgia Ryle, Donna Townsend, Eve Osborne, Dawn Hasiotis, and Tammy Baughman.

Chapter 1

I've never had any desire to be known as a bar hop but that seems the perfect, if unfortunate, tag considering my path through this town tonight. Not that any fault can be laid at my feet or, rather, my paws. In point of fact, trailing a young woman whose name I don't know from bar to bar can't really be called hopping, at all. Rabbits hop. Cats don't. Still, that phrase, along with the image, is fixed in my mind.

Luckily, up to this point, we haven't strayed far from where I left my human, Dax. Unluckily, I have a feeling that's about to change. I did, at least, make sure to catch his eye as I exited the small bar and grill where we treated ourselves to better than average burgers and fries. With that shared look, Dax will know I'm out and about and that I'll find him when I'm done. We have a good understanding of each other in that regard.

We've just arrived in this little college town so I don't know my way around as well as I will after a few days of exploring. Dax has already found work of the temporary kind that he prefers, so I know we'll be here for more than a day or two. This visit to the state of North Carolina might be my favorite in our roaming so far. The scenic drives have been true to their names with the first hints of spring budding out in the trees and bushes along the roadsides. Of course, for us, it's walk or hitch a ride, and the view is all the better for that!

The interiors of the bars I've passed through in order to keep a watchful eye on this young woman don't hold the same appeal. Not seedy. I've seen seedy a time or two. For the most part, they've all been crowded with human adults enjoying their evening a little too much. I'm not a fan of the odor of alcohol, not in a glass or, worse, seeping through the pores of those who do. Some enjoy it a little too much and aren't steady on their feet. Their weaving path can make picking my way through them tricky.

That description fits my self-imposed charge for the night. I noticed that much as soon as I saw her get to her feet and knew I couldn't let her walk out into the night without a bodyguard. I'd watched her wine glass be refilled too often while her plate remained half-full. Worse, she'd attracted the wrong kind of attention, even in the quiet place Dax and I had chosen to find a solid meal.

The young guy who took hold of her arm as she passed his table let it go fast enough when she said something I've learned is considered unflattering. The next guy might not be so easy to put in his place.

* * *

Wolf Stockton leaned against the bar. The beer in his hand had grown warm, but he wasn't there to get drunk. His gaze followed the girl as she twirled slowly across the dance floor and not because she was drop-dead gorgeous—

not, in truth, because of her looks at all. He watched her because she was a problem waiting to happen, and when she became a problem, the problem would become his. He'd rather derail that train than deal with the aftermath of a head-on crash.

In the murky glow of neon, she stood out like moonlight. The sleeveless, white dress hugged her every curve. He didn't recognize her, and Albrecht was his town. She might have come in with the reenactors, but she didn't seem to fit with that crowd. He'd done some studying when he'd first learned what was to befall Albrecht. His digging had been somewhat reassuring. Those enthralled with historical reenactments were held to be a serious-minded bunch, going to the same venues year after year, never causing any problem, rarely partying down. The history buffs who attended to watch the painstakingly recreated historical events were categorized the same, at least for the most part. This girl, however, seemed hell-bent on having a grand time and without help from anyone else.

She'd caught his eye when she came through the door, opening the small bag that hung across her shoulder and handing the doorman a handful of crumpled bills. Like the professional he was, the bouncer at the door had counted what was owed into the cashbox then handed the rest back to her, stamping her wrist and shaking his head as she'd moved straight to the dance floor. She'd snagged a glass of wine from the tray of a passing waitress without the server even realizing it was gone. That's when Wolf Stockton had realized the need to keep an eye on her as, glass in hand, she executed some slow, dreamy dance moves all by her lonesome while couples swept around her. He was relieved when she finished the pilfered wine and placed the empty glass on the corner of a table that also wasn't hers. At least broken glass wouldn't be added to the mess when it came. She ignored, or never even noticed, the startled *hey* of protest from one of the table's occupants.

She'd have been trouble enough sober. And she wasn't sober.

His wasn't the only attention she snared, but she remained oblivious until a cocky dude in frayed jeans and a black tee shirt eased close and slid an arm around her waist. Wolf tensed, ready to step in, when her slim, bare arm showed an unexpected flash of strength and well-toned muscle. Cocky dude found himself sprawled butt-down on the dance floor. To Wolf's relief, the guy took it well, dusting himself off and laughing as he walked back to his table. His buddies continued to rib him for the next few minutes, spurring another of them to push his chair back and swagger toward the tangle of dancers as the music and her moves kicked up a beat.

With a sigh, Wolf made his way to the edge of the floor in front of the band. Sure enough, the dumbass reached for the girl when she got close enough, but this one was better prepared for a show of strength. He wrapped his arms around her, pinning her arms to her side, nuzzling his chin close to her cheek. "Come on, honey. One dance. I've got a hundred bucks on it."

"Hope you can afford to lose it, asshole." Her voice slurred a little on the words. Wolf noted she didn't bother asking him to loosen his grip. The heel of her cute little boot with lots of fringe came down on his instep, and a second later her knee rammed his crotch. His howl stopped the band, and Wolf stopped *him* by the simple act of snaring the collar of his casual button-down shirt and twisting until it caught said asshole's Adam's apple as well as his attention.

Wolf handed the guy off to the bouncer who'd made his way through the small crowd. The band resumed playing, and Wolf turned to the young woman who watched him with solemn eyes. For a moment, she reminded him of someone, but he was certain he'd never seen her before. He held out his hand to her. "Dance?"

"I don't dance with men."

"Think of me as one of the girls," he suggested.

A faint smile curved her lips as her glance swept him. "Don't know that my imagination is that good."

"One dance and sit at my table. I'll leave you alone but so will every guy in here, I promise."

She lifted a perfectly arched brow. "Think well of yourself, don't you?"

"Well enough."

She reached up to touch his hair where it brushed against his collar. He hadn't made time for the trim it needed. "Are you a bad boy?"

He gave a humorless laugh. "Not even close."

To his surprise, she stepped closer. *I don't dance with men*, she'd said. As she draped her slender curves against him, he couldn't help but think it a shame if he didn't have a chance with her. Not that he needed a woman in his life because he sure as hell didn't, but a shame even so.

She danced with him as she'd danced alone, with fluidity and grace and damn little inhibition. By the time the song ended, he wasn't sure it was dark enough that he could step away from her without every single guy in there knowing what he was feeling. Then again, safest for her if they did know.

True to his word, he left her alone after that. She sat at his table and drank or danced when a song drew her to the floor. He made one attempt to pay for her drinks, and the look she cut him when she said *no* forestalled a second try.

When the waitress told them it was last call, she made a moue of disappointment and shook her head. "I'm not done dancing. Gotta find someplace else to go."

Wolf touched her hand. "I can promise there isn't another bar open now. Not in this town." He stood. "If you don't want another drink, how about one last dance?"

She surprised him again when she took the hand he held out to her and let him tug her to her feet. He wasn't, however, surprised when she swayed. Although she'd had no more than two glasses of wine while she'd sat at his table, he doubted even she knew how many she'd had before that. He stifled a groan at the surge of pure lust he felt when she leaned into him and looped her arms around his neck. If she wore a bra, he couldn't tell. Her hair smelled like clean rainfall. She whisper-sang every word of the song in a soft, husky voice that he suspected was above average on a bad day. Today wasn't a bad day. It was a love song and not a happy one. He was relieved when the song ended, and the lights in the room brightened.

Most often this would be the moment when a guy got his first good look at a girl he'd hooked up with for the night. Some would be a disappointment. Some wouldn't. This girl was no disappointment. Not that it would matter either way. He wasn't on the make, and they weren't hooking up for the night.

She blinked up at him with sleepy eyes and smiled. "I'm Kylah. You can take me home."

Aw, hell.

* * *

This can't be good. Despite the fact that the gentleman appears to be just that—a gentleman—I'm not naïve enough to allow Kylah, as I now know her name to be, to leave with him unaccompanied. I'm way too familiar with the male of any species. I'll need to continue my protection at least a little while longer. I've managed to remain unnoticed so far. Most humans make surveillance all too easy with their lack of awareness of their surroundings. It's that same lack that helps to make them vulnerable to dangers that lurk around them.

It may take some maneuvering on my part to not get left behind. That's not a major step for me. It won't be my first episode as a stowaway, and I suspect it won't be my last. I have many talents.

Here we go then, out the door of the dance joint and into the night air. I nod approval when her escort keeps a careful eye on her progress. A time or two he steadies her with a light hand at her waist but removes it once she regains her equilibrium. That confirms my thoughts that he really is a gentleman.

She stops in her tracks, when he opens the passenger door of a dark truck. "That's not my truck."

"No, it's mine. If you trust me with the keys, I'll have yours delivered wherever you need it in the morning."

Recognizing the unyielding tone, I slip into the back seat. She's not going to be allowed behind the wheel of any vehicle. It might be she's familiar with that tone as well, but I'm still a little surprised when she shrugs and steps up into the vehicle. I hope she doesn't make a practice of that. I have her back at the moment, but she has no way of knowing that. I'm reassured by the trappings inside the vehicle, including the blue light on the dash that identifies it as unmarked law enforcement. All in all, the truck fits well with the vibes I pick up from this man.

Her escort steps in on the driver's side, and the engine catches with a purring sound. He pauses the vehicle at the intersection. "Which way?"

I peer over the console as she opens her purse and hands him a small card sheathed in a tiny envelope. I recognize it as a hotel key. It's not like the keys for the rooms at the Hotel Warm Springs, but it's still a key. Don't ask me how it works. I'm a cat. Dax and I don't stay in hotels, but I've seen one before.

He gives a huff of exasperation. "For all you know, I could be a serial killer."

She turns her head to look at him. "For all you know, I could too."

I'm not surprised that his second huff of exasperation is tinged with amusement. She's a bit of a smartass. I know one when I hear one.

The drive to her hotel was short but enough for a drunk girl to fall asleep.

* * *

Wolf put the vehicle in park and killed the ignition, then sat staring at the female who'd crashed, not drifted, into sleep. She was sure a looker, but she was just as big a mess. He tried to rouse her with little success, but then he hadn't expected much, a major reason he was parked at the back entrance. The last thing he needed was to be seen carrying an unconscious female into a hotel. He tucked her room key into his shirt pocket, then stepped out of the truck and walked around to the passenger side.

He opened the door and stood for a moment looking down at her. It'd be a hell of a lot better if she could walk under her own steam, but he didn't hold out much hope of that happening. "Kylah."

"Hmmm."

"Kylah, wake up."

When her response was to snuggle deeper into the soft leather seat, he sighed and unhooked her seatbelt to lift her. Her weight took him by surprise given the slenderness of her form until he recalled the strength she'd displayed in dealing with her unwelcome admirers on the dance floor. Muscle weighed more than fat, not that she had an ounce of that on her. Turning, he shoved the passenger door with his shoulder to close it, then nearly dropped the girl in his arms as a flash of solid gray fur leapt from the back seat, landing on the sidewalk at his feet. He stifled a curse as he and the cat stared at each other. This was a night of surprises.

The cat followed him up the walk and to the glass door where Wolf didn't even attempt to keep the feline from entering. Luck was with him, and the hallway was empty. Rather than pushing that luck, he took the stairs, the cat a silent partner in the climb to the third floor. By the time they reached the door that matched the number on the hotel cardkey, Wolf had reason to be grateful he lived a life that kept him physically fit.

With a secure hold on the sleeping beauty in his arms, he fished the room key from his pocket. It took some maneuvering to get the door open while the light flashed green, but he managed. And the cat sauntered into the room with him.

The room proved to be a suite with a tiny kitchenette and sitting area. Moving past that, he walked into a bedroom neat as a pin. Somehow, he hadn't expected that. Whoever she was and whatever she was doing in town, her stay didn't appear to be a short one. Stacks of jeans and

tee shirts, some long-sleeved and some short-sleeved, lined
the top of the long, low dresser. No less than three pair of
riding boots stood side by side under the desk.

Not that any of this was his business. He placed her as
far to the center of the bed as possible and watched as she
turned on her side and curled into a ball. Morning wasn't
likely to be kind to her.

When Wolf turned to leave the room, the cat stood in
his path. He was sleek and gray and had gold-colored eyes
that gleamed in the low lighting of the lamp by the bed.
"What?"

The cat, of course, did not answer. Though not a cat
enthusiast, Wolf couldn't help but admire the fact that the
creature had managed to remain with his owner undetected.
If the cat were a dog, Wolf could have believed he had her
protection in mind. That thought led him to remember
that the cat's owner was now here without a vehicle. With a
little luck, she might remember where she left it when she
woke up.

He picked up the pen and pad left on every hotel
nightstand, wrote his number and a brief note, and signed
his name. That was the best he could do for now. Ignoring
her cat, who still watched his every move with suspicion,
he walked out. As he heard the lock click when he closed
the door behind him, he realized he didn't even know her
last name.

* * *

Kylah bolted to an upright position as her phone
alarm jangled. Her heart and her head pounded with equal
unpleasantness as she took stock of her surroundings

and struggled with the fact that her phone seemed to be attached to her chest. No, not attached, concealed in the tiny clutch with a strap she wore over her neck and one shoulder when she didn't want to keep up with anything heavier. She managed to unwind it from around her upper body, retrieve the phone, and hit stop on the alarm.

Eight a.m. She'd reset it two hours past normal before leaving the hotel room last night, not honestly believing she'd sleep in but hopeful anyway. Time to shower, eat— if she could—and drive to the county's fairground barn. The shower was a must, but she suspected breakfast wasn't going to be very high on her list. The pounding in her chest had eased but not the pounding in her head, and when she rolled over her heart did too.

Her shriek startled the cat as much as the sight of him had startled her, but he was altogether more stoic. He ducked his head and his ears, oddly folded at the ends, flattened, but that golden gaze was unwavering, and he never changed body position. He sat regally on the hotel dresser beside the television she had yet to turn on and doubted she ever would, though she'd be here at least two weeks. She leaned her head into her hands and closed her eyes. She was never, ever drinking again, so help her, but when she looked again, the cat was still there.

Moving to the edge of the bed, she slid to her feet and muttered, "If you're gonna be dumb, you've gotta be tough." She hoped she'd had fun. She wished she could remember it. Particularly since that was going to be her last attempt at being a party animal. Even at the wry thought, the familiar, faint sorrow swept through her. It was time to let go. She knew that.

The hotel bathroom was standard size and adequate.

She turned the shower to the hottest setting, then stripped and stepped in, leaning her head against the tile as the steam rose up around her. She didn't turn off the water until it began to cool.

It wasn't until after she'd showered that she found the note on the nightstand and realized she had no idea how she spent her evening, where she left her truck, or how she got in her room. And she was beholden to someone named Wolf.

The cat seemed the least of her troubles.

She sank to the edge of the bed with her phone and entered the number on the note with a rare-for-her reluctance. She either did things or she didn't do them. She didn't do them hesitantly. Until now. To her relief, she got a recorded message. The strong, masculine voice caused her eyes to close again. Mother Mary, what had she done?

She cleared her throat and took a deep breath before answering. "It seems you got me back to my room last night. I appreciate that and the offer of help but I can find my truck. And you left your cat. I'm not much of a cat person so—ah—you'll need to come get him. Or her."

She ended the call then voiced a series of curses that even the cat seemed to understand as he uncoiled from his comfortable position on one of the pillows and sat upright, giving her an indignant stare. Most of the words she'd never said in public or even aloud in private, but sometimes …

"May as well get this show on the road." She glanced at the cat. "You included, but you'll have to walk and keep up." She could imagine the uproar if the housekeeping staff found a cat in her room.

Getting dressed in jeans and a tee shirt took little time.

Her hair would have to air dry, and she could care less about makeup when she'd be covered in dust within the first few hours of her day.

With a frustrated glance at the time, she made another phone call, setting it to hands-free while she pulled on socks and boots. She started talking as soon as he answered. "Jake, I'm running late, but we'll get started as soon as I get there."

Jake was her right hand, on the road and on the job. Not for anyone else would she give up the comfortable living quarters of her trailer for a hotel room. She despised hotel rooms. And not for anyone but Kylah would Jake leave his comfortable bunk room attached to her barn back home.

"No, problem," Jake answered, "but you might want to get here sooner rather than later if you can."

"Why? Is something wrong?" There was. She could hear it in his voice. But it wasn't the horses, or he would have called her before she could call him.

"I'm not sure what's going on but there's a dozen or so blue light specials here and a uniform around every corner."

"I'm on my way."

As soon as she figured out where the hell she'd left her truck.

* * *

Not a cat person? Hmph. It'll be a while before I forgive that insult. Regardless, this Kylah, for all her grit, she has the saddest eyes of any human I've ever seen, and if she's walking into a police situation, my services may still be needed, in spite of her rudeness.

Chapter 2

Wolf propped his elbows on the hood of his truck, ignoring the fact that it needed washing, which meant his dark shirt would soon be some shade of dust. He was off duty. He was tired. But he'd been called, so he was here. For the past half hour or so, he'd been watching sheriff's deputies milling around the trucks and trailers and RV's cluttering the grounds, which had been reserved for the next couple of weeks. The upcoming First Reenactment of The Battle of Albrecht Creek was generating as much excitement as the groundbreaking for their first casino had done years back.

"Stockton."

Wolf turned at the sound of his name. He and Sheriff Mitchell weren't enemies, but they damned sure weren't friends, either. They had a history, and it hadn't always been a good one. Which was one of several reasons he'd made it a point to come when asked. The request had been made in polite terms, which was an oddity all by itself.

"Les." Wolf offered the greeting without moving a muscle more than necessary. "What've you got?"

After a moment, the sheriff sighed then removed his sunglasses. Wolf stifled a faint smile and did the same. He knew it was juvenile powerplay but, all things considered, it still gave him a small measure of satisfaction. It hadn't been easy being a teen under Les Mitchell's thirty-year reign in law enforcement. Sheriff Mitchell wasn't a big or blustery man, but he was a strong one, and the worn adage *talk softly but carry a big stick* had been created for men like him.

Les rubbed a calloused hand over his trim mustache before answering the question. "A dead body."

Wolf straightened, pushing away from the hood of his truck. "On the Boundary?" The Qualla Boundary was a land trust comprised of properties held by the Eastern Band of the Cherokee, not all of whom were happy with the idea of troupes of reenactors invading the land adjacent to theirs.

"Off. About halfway between the fairgrounds and there."

Nothing but sparse woods out there, Wolf thought.

"And?" As in why had the sheriff called him? Why was he here and not still sprawled across his bed, where he'd toppled after taking a drunk girl to her hotel and leaving her alone in safety, when he'd have preferred stripping her down to what he suspected might be some very sexy underwear. But that's not what he did with drunk girls. Not since he'd been—oh—nineteen years stupid and equally drunk. Not anymore, no matter how willing the girl.

"You aren't here officially, of course."

Of course. Wolf waited without expression. He was a master of the skill.

"See, the problem is that the dead body is a woman. And one of your kids says he found her, called it in."

Wolf's gut clenched. "Who?" He worked with several at-risk teens in an after-school program. Some of them were more at risk than the others.

"Case."

"Where is he now?"

"Back of my squad car."

Crap, he had to be terrified. "Come on, Les. You know damned well that kid didn't kill anyone." He hadn't missed the way Les had phrased it. Not *found her* but *says he found her.*

"I'm not looking at him real hard, but I won't rule it out yet. Thing is, Wolf, he's holding something back or flat-out lying. I'm hoping he'll tell you what he won't tell me."

Wolf rubbed the back of his neck. This was a helluva way to start his day. "You call his folks?"

"Talked with his dad, who said I could keep him--one less mouth to feed." Les shook his head and added, "His mom took off again a couple of days ago. Not answering her phone."

Damn it. "I'll talk to him."

He started toward the squad car, turning back when Les said his name.

"There's one other problem." Les looked even more pained than he had a moment earlier.

Of course, there was. Wolf waited without comment for the other shoe to drop.

"The deceased is one of the reenactors."

Well, hell. "Does Rita know yet?"

Rita was Wolf's ex-wife and the sheriff's baby sister. Of greater importance, she chaired the history department at the College of the Carolinas Albrecht Campus and was *the* driving force behind the First Reenactment of the Battle of Albrecht Creek. Any negative publicity was going to make her unhappy. A murder was going to send her over the wall.

"Nope. I thought you could drive out to see her after you talk with the kid and give her a heads up."

"In return for which?" If Les wanted to dump the unpleasant chore on him, negotiations were in order.

"I keep you in the loop on the investigation. Maybe bring you in on an official basis."

It was a deal made in hell, and one Les knew Wolf wouldn't turn down. The fact that Wolf was cross-deputized with the sheriff's department didn't mean Les *had* to keep him informed or allow him to take part. It meant he could if he wanted. "I don't suppose that's all you're going to want for that favor."

"Well, I hope this was one outsider killing off another and that I don't have to look toward the Boundary."

There was a big, silent *but* at the end of that sentence. If the investigation turned its ugly head in that direction, the fact that Wolf was a Deputy of the Cherokee Nation Marshal Service would be as crucial as the fact that he was a trusted member of the Nation's Emergency Management team. And just plain trusted. Wolf decided to push back a little.

"I'll talk with Rita but I'm on the case. Officially."

Les hesitated, then nodded without any sign of rancor. "I'll make that call today."

Because the sheriff wasn't irritated at the demand, Wolf knew he'd planned to do that anyway. Which—damn it—meant he'd wasted a high card he could've played later.

"What happened to the safety rules, including no live ammunition on the grounds?"

"Since when do murderers follow the rules?" Les retorted.

"Any chance it was an accident?"

Les shook his head. "Nope. Not unless she shot herself through the heart with what I suspect was a vintage rifle."

"Last night?"

"Not likely. Animals hadn't got to her yet. Coroner will have to place time of death, but my guess is sometime around daylight."

Wolf grunted, thinking hard. "You said halfway between here and the Boundary. Any idea what she was doing in the middle of those woods that time of morning?"

"Looks as if that's where she chose to set up camp."

"Alone?"

Les nodded. "Appears that way for now. Damned lunatic reenactors. I told Rita this was a bad idea."

Wolf slid his sunglasses back in place. "Well, if I were you, I sure as hell wouldn't say I told you so."

Les gave a humorless snort of laughter. "Give me a call after you talk to her. And get a damned haircut, why don't you."

"Sure. And I'll tell Rita you sent best wishes."

The telling response Wolf got for his verbal jab was a flip of a middle finger as the sheriff spun on one heel and stalked toward the two deputies heading his way.

* * *

Wolf opened the back door of the sheriff's car and leaned in. The teen was huddled into his light camo jacket, hands in his lap, which meant Wolf wouldn't have to blast Les for handcuffing the kid. Case glanced up at Wolf before fixing his gaze down at his hands once more. But Wolf had seen the lack of welcome in those dark brown eyes. Still, the boy scooted over when Wolf slid in, leaving the door open to the sunlight beyond.

"Talk," Wolf said. He was firm, but he kept his voice quiet.

"Ain't much to say. I told Sheriff Mitchell I found that woman." Wolf watched Case's hands clench and unclench. "I didn't touch her. Didn't need to. She was already dead."

Wolf knew the sixteen-year-old wouldn't lie to him, but he agreed with Les, Case was leaving something out, something he thought was important or even potentially damning.

"What were you doing in those woods?" He kept his tone light and non-threatening.

"Walking."

"Kinda early for a morning stroll. Best I recall mornings aren't your thing." That was Case's excuse any time Wolf suggested a sunrise fishing trip. A few of the others would go, but Case wasn't one to roll out of bed unless it was a school day. He never missed class.

Case cut him a quick look but didn't say anything to that.

"Were you running away, again?"

"No, sir."

Wolf decided to cut to the chase. He could sit here all day playing twenty questions, but he suspected the kid could outlast him. On a good day, Case might even outwit him. He was like his mama, smart as a whip, one of the many reasons his father, who wasn't half as smart, couldn't manage him. And the man resented it to hell and gone, using his fists when words failed.

"What are you hiding, Case? And don't tell me *nothing*. Tell me the truth." He still didn't raise his voice, but he sharpened it to the no-nonsense tone he sometimes had to use with each and every one of the teens he worked with on a regular basis. They weren't his kids, but he treated them as if they were, as he hoped he would have his own.

Case met him look for look then shook his head.

"If you don't give me something to help you, the sheriff's going to keep looking your way until the killer is found."

"Reckon he'll have to keep looking then."

Wolf sighed. Whatever Case was hiding was important to him, important enough he wasn't going to open up to anyone about it. But Wolf could see the fear behind his determination. That meant Wolf had to make sure the sheriff solved this case fast, before Case ran off again, before he ran so far no one could find him this time. Wolf's greatest concern, greater even than Case's flight risk, was what had frightened him. Who or what had he seen?

He stepped back out of the car, his action followed by Case's worried gaze. As aggravated as he was at the boy's stubbornness, he wasn't going to leave him fearful and feeling alone. Wouldn't risk making him desperate.

"I've got an errand to run. I'll talk to the sheriff before I leave and get you released to me if he's not willing to let you go home."

Case nodded, looking a little less anxious. "I need to go home, Wolf. I help with the younger ones. So, they don't get in trouble at home."

Wolf knew what he meant. He was their shield from the man who'd provided the sperm, but had never learned how to be a father. Knew nothing about being a real man. He nodded, "I'll do what I can, there, too. Don't worry about going to jail, okay? Not going to happen."

Wolf caught up with Les and gave him an update on his exchange with the teen. Les grudgingly agreed he didn't have any reason to hold Case as yet but voiced Wolf's own concern. "That kid's not telling all he knows. He knows something or he saw something. Either way, keeping it a secret could get him killed."

Wolf couldn't argue the point. Not if whoever pulled that trigger got wind that Case had seen something. Or already knew that he had.

Les' expression turned hopeful. "You going to see Rita now?"

"Yeah, I'll check in with you later, see if I need to give Case a ride home."

"No need. I'll owe you that much. I'll get him home and make sure his dad knows he's not in trouble. I'll be waiting to hear what Rita has to say."

Wolf rolled his eyes and walked toward his truck. Hand on the door, he paused at the sound of a familiar voice raised in anger. Curious, he changed course. He was not in any hurry for the talk with his ex. Instead, he headed in the direction of that voice, toward a long, fancy looking horse trailer pulled alongside one of the long barns. Grant Edmunds, one of the leading reenactment organizers from the college, was giving some poor fellow a blistering set-down but didn't seem to be making much of an impression.

The guy he berated tipped his cowboy hat back and

crossed his arms over his chest. He wore his well-washed jeans and work shirt like a comfortable second skin. His average build and weight looked unimpressive against Grant's above average height and bulk. But the cowboy, himself, didn't look much impressed with Grant. "There's legal hookups here," he said laconically.

"Flyers were given out to everyone bringing livestock. Among other things, it outlined the requirement to park at the rear. Seems like you're the only one who didn't get that message, mister."

"My name's Jake. No mister needed. Ms. Kylah told me to park and sleep here, next to the horses."

"I don't give a flying rat's ass what your Ms. Kylah told you." Grant leaned back in order to see past the freightliner and read the inscription emblazoned on the side of the trailer. K.T. West Equine. "You tell Mr. West to get in touch with me at once. That's who has the contract, and that's the person I'm going to deal with."

Jake nodded toward a silver pickup moving at more than the legal speed in their direction. "Wait a second or so and you can deliver that message yourself."

With an eye on the dust cloud thrown up by heavy-duty wheels, Wolf doubted the *or so* would be needed. Those wheels didn't exactly slide to a stop at their feet— but close. He had one thought as the driver stepped out wearing a nondescript knit shirt with tight fitting jeans and no makeup. She was still a problem waiting to happen.

Even with her eyes shielded by oversized sunglasses, Wolf had no problem recognizing her. Because her attention was fixed on the two men squared off in front of her, he had plenty of time to see things he hadn't noticed in the low light of the bar. Things like the farmer's tan.

The top she wore sported a scoop neck and her tan line was more a vee. Glints of gold threaded her hair and he doubted any bottle produced that shine. But what did he know about hair products, he asked himself. But that body? That was exactly as he remembered.

And so was the cat who leaped to the ground beside her.

She didn't glance his way as far as he could tell with her eyes hidden by those shades. Grant hadn't noticed him either, which Wolf considered a good thing.

* * *

"Kylah, this gentleman would like to talk with you." Jake gestured toward the man glaring at him.

Kylah studied Jake's sun-browned face a moment trying to determine why he'd called her Kylah. He didn't seem aggravated with her. She trusted him more than she did any other person in her life. She also knew him better than any other person in her life. They'd been friends and work partners a while now. Despite the fact that he wasn't smiling, he seemed more entertained than stressed. She relaxed her spine and turned her attention to the gentleman in question, who spoke up in quick response to Jake's words.

"Actually, no. I prefer to speak to the owner."

"Okay." She extended her hand. "What can I help you with?"

He was all of six feet and more, which meant she had to look up at him, but that was fine. She didn't intimidate easily. Actually, not at all.

He stared at her. "You're K.T. West?"

"I am. Or Kylah, if you prefer. And you are …?

"Dean Edmunds."

For a moment, the first name confused her. She recognized Edmunds but Dean wasn't what she recalled from their correspondence. Then she realized he'd introduced himself with his title rather than his first name. Dean Grant Edmunds. How pompous of him. She gave him a slow look. Thinning blond hair, pale green eyes. A bit out of shape if she had to guess. Not that he had a paunch. He didn't. What he did have was a softness about him.

"You wanted to speak with me?" she reminded him. Her headache had quieted to a tolerable level, thanks to coffee and a muffin. The cat had consumed her omelet on the drive from the hotel. Spinach, mushrooms, and all.

"Yes." He still seemed somewhat disconcerted by the fact that K.T. West was a female. "Trailers aren't allowed to be parked next to the barn."

"Why not?"

"It's the rule."

That answer didn't impress her. While she wouldn't call herself a deliberate rule-breaker, she didn't abide by them unless they made very good sense. This one didn't, as far as she could tell. "Whose rule is it?"

"Mine." He looked dumbfounded at being questioned. His fair skin took on a red tinge, and she gathered this was a man who disliked confrontation in any guise, preferring people to obey without question.

"Either Jake or myself must be close to the horses at all times. He sleeps in that trailer, so I'm not moving it."

"I've laid things out very orderly so as to avoid clutter and chaos. I'm afraid I'll have to require you to move."

Kylah looked at Jake. "Hook up, and we'll load up. With luck, we can be home faster than we got here."

"What—no—you can't." Edmunds was brick red now. "I'll sue for breach. We have a contract."

She smiled. "Actually, we don't. I brought it with me, and it's going to leave with me in that trailer I'm about to get moved for you."

Edmunds hesitated before asking, "Can we speak in private, Ms. West?"

"Sure." She glanced around. There was no one within hearing distance except Jake and a well-built guy in tee shirt and jeans, wearing dark, dark sunshades. Muscles without bulk, a strong jaw, high cheekbones, and a blade-thin nose. Once upon a time, the description *sexy* would have popped into her mind. But that was then and this was now. He didn't look interested in their exchange, probably one of the organizers waiting to speak with the dean. "We can step into the living quarters of my trailer. Excuse us, Jake."

The dean—and the cat—followed her into the trailer where she gestured toward the bench seat. "You may as well sit down or you'll end up hitting your head." She slid her sunglasses to the top of her head, the better to see in the dim interior, and propped one hip against the counter.

He took her suggestion and sat but launched right into his argument. "I'm sure you can understand the need for close attention to detail in an effort this large."

"I can understand your nervousness about it," she conceded. "I believe this is your first reenactment. Or at least the first for your college."

"My wife and I are ardent reenactors and have been for some years. Those experiences as a participant have been invaluable in helping me … ah … helping us plan for this event. I can't have everyone parking wherever they please. We worked weeks on our logistics plan."

Since he hadn't asked a question, she didn't offer anything in response. He frowned at the brief silence. Like so many people, it seemed he didn't like a vacuum and couldn't avoid filling it. That almost always worked in her favor.

"I'm paying you a small fortune," he reminded her.

"You would be, yes, but my horses are worth that fortune. And so am I. I'm leading three big scenes for you," she reminded. "The first cavalry charge with jumps—that's the easy one—but dramatic so it will be a fan favorite. The second charge when my horse is shot from under me, tricky for amateurs but not for me or my horse. And the battle scene where my horse plays dead while I shoot over his side. My horses will grab and hold the attention of the spectators because they, and I, are damned good at what we do." When he met her comments with silence, she pushed away from the counter and reached for the door. "Seems we're not going to move past this impasse. I'm sure you have better things to do, and so do I."

"Wait! Wait," he repeated the word more quietly. He let out long breath. "Okay."

"Okay?" She lifted a brow.

"The trailer can stay where it is. But I want that contract in my hand today."

"I can work with that." She held out one hand and ignored the reluctance with which he shook it. Some people, men more often than women in her experience, didn't take defeat with a good nature. Then again, some men simply didn't like shaking hands with women, as if that acknowledged them on equal footing. Which they already were.

She opened the trailer door, waiting until he and the cat stepped out before she followed. "So, any particular reason we're surrounded by law enforcement?" She'd noted a mix of vehicles which appeared to represent everyone from city police to sheriff deputies to university officers. A mix she found very odd.

"There was an unfortunate incident in the area this morning, sometime around daylight."

"Unfortunate how?"

"A death. Accidental, I'm sure," he added hastily. "And, even if it proves otherwise, it didn't occur on the fairgrounds proper. I'm sure you'll all be safe here. But doubtless the authorities will be poking about and interviewing everyone who might have been in the area at the time, including your help and you, Ms. West."

Before she could speak, a movement to one side of her trailer caught her attention. The man she'd noticed earlier stepped closer, coming face to face with the dean. Even from behind the dark shades he wore, she could feel his gaze sweep over her. But it was to Dean Edmunds that he spoke.

"It won't be necessary for anyone to question Ms. West." His words dropped into the sudden silence. "I'll speak with the sheriff."

"Wolf," the dean said, "I didn't realize you were here."

Kylah closed her eyes as the two talked quietly for a moment. The face hadn't been familiar but the voice was unmistakably that from the recorded message on the number she'd called earlier. *If you're gonna be dumb*, she reminded herself as she opened her eyes and slid her sunglasses back in place. She didn't finish the thought. She didn't need to.

She couldn't have cared less about the curious glance the dean sent her way as he was leaving, but she did care about Jake's lengthier perusal as he stepped to one side to wait for her. Jake kept up with dates, had known that yesterday was tough for her. She didn't need him fretting about why a man he'd never seen thought he could speak on Kylah's behalf.

Forcing a light tone to her voice, she smiled at the stranger. "I guess you've come for your cat."

He smiled faintly. "That's something we'll need to talk about. He's not my cat."

* * *

Wolf watched Kylah's reaction to that statement.

"What do you mean he's not your cat?"

He suspected she was glaring at him behind those dark shades, but there wasn't much else he could say, so he repeated the words. "He's not my cat."

She lowered her voice. "Then how did he get in my room?"

"The same way he got in my truck when I took you *back* to your room."

She blew out a breath. "I do appreciate you getting me off the streets. Drinking isn't my thing, so I'm sure I made a fool of myself."

"Not unless you count putting two jackasses in their place—on the dance floor."

He could tell his comment gave her pause, but when she slid those sunglasses to the top of her head, her action gave *him* pause. More than that, he took a punch to the gut.

In the dark of the bar, he'd thought her eyes were blue or maybe gray. They were neither. Or both.

For the first time, he could tell she wasn't as young as he'd thought. Last night, he'd judged her to be early twenties, which put her squarely off limits to him. Now he thought early to mid-thirties. Neon had given her beauty a touch of delicacy. Sunlight revealed the strength in high cheekbones and the line of her jaw. Still beautiful but far from delicate. And not off limits.

And not happy at the idea that she'd been the center of a scene. He stifled a smile at her faint frown of chagrin. She wouldn't appreciate it.

"K.T.?"

The cowboy had walked up with a quiet that Wolf had to respect. He'd heard him but knew he might not have if he hadn't seen him first. He was that quiet. Despite his slight limp.

"Hey, Jake. Ready to get to work?"

"Yes, ma'am. I've got the roan and the bay saddled."

She smiled. "They've got names, Jake."

"Yes, ma'am."

Wolf suspected this was a frequent exchange. When she glanced back his way, he touched the brim of his cap. "Looks like we've all got work to do."

For the first time, he saw a look of faint curiosity cross her face but she didn't give voice to it. "Thanks again, Mister …"

"Stockton. Wolf Stockton." He wasn't there in an official capacity—yet—so he didn't bother with a title. His glance included Jake as he added, "You'll want to keep a close watch around you for now."

The other man gave him a look that spoke volumes,

but Wolf wasn't going to apologize for the suggestion.

Wolf turned to leave and found himself face to face with the gray cat. With a quick sidestep, he kept going. No way was he going to become caregiver to a cat.

Chapter 3

*W*olf, that's an odd name for a man. And, from what I saw and heard, a person used to assuming command. 'I'll speak to the sheriff' he told that Edmunds guy, as if that would make things right. The minute I heard that whole exchange, I knew my instincts were on target. Edmunds may try to reassure everyone that the death was accidental, but a heavy presence of the law indicates there's more thought to the contrary. Regardless of any attraction Wolf might feel to Kylah, and I suspect he does, a dead body practically on her doorstep—or in this case trailer step—begs for snooping around by someone impartial. And I'm just the cat to do it, but not only because I find nosing about an entertaining way to pass the time. I actually do have some experience, especially in my recent ramblings with my pal, Dax.

No time like the present, I decide, as Wolf heads to his truck and Kylah walks toward the barn with Jake. My attention is drawn to an unmarked car pulling to a stop. Two uniformed individuals step out of the vehicle, and I move closer as they open the trunk and begin removing equipment bags. Bingo, I've grabbed the brass ring. Yeah, I know, I'm mixing metaphors but still dead right as these newcomers are crime scene investigators. Their arrival is confirmation of my suspicions, so the pair of them are exactly who I need to shadow.

As we strike out toward the hills beyond, I'm immediately disappointed by both the pace, which seems slow to me, and the exchange between the two.

The trouble with humans is that they see what they expect to see and aren't often spurred to pursue the unexpected. That's one shortcoming on a list too long to catalog at the present. Then again, I'll admit I've had the pleasure of working around several intelligent humans while I busy myself cracking cases. And, while I don't care for bias in any form, the majority of those intelligent ones have been females. Like me, they seem to find the hows and the whys of crime an interesting puzzle.

Case in point, of the two I trail, the woman seems to be the more astute. It may be that she's the more seasoned professional, but she's the one who notices me traipsing along with them. Her male counterpart remains oblivious. I don't fault her just because she doesn't see the significance of my presence…yet. I am disappointed that she, like her partner, seems more interested in discussing motive before they've established the physical attributes of the death. They're already speculating it to be a crime of passion rather than robbery, and only because the victim was female. Sure, there could be merit to that thought. Then again, there are merits to other possibilities as well. We'll see, but I won't rush to judgement, and I don't think they should either.

When we reach our destination, it looks an unlikely place for anyone to be tromping about in expensive jewelry or carrying a *significant amount of cash. But those aren't the only things people consider valuable enough to steal. Guns for example. For a few minutes, we pause to look around. Taking the lay of the land is always a good first step. The ground slopes in what looks like a natural clearing where we stand, but the surrounding hills are more rugged and covered in scrub trees.*

I note that someone has marked the perimeter of the crime scene. Not a bad job, I think to myself. The investigators exchange greetings with the two sheriff's deputies standing guard then duck under the barricade of tape which surrounds a tent, stool, and table with various paraphernalia that appear to be very old-fashioned in nature. I feel as if I've stepped onto a movie set. Not a city set like in the Dirty Harry movies ... more like a wilderness adventure. Maybe I should add antiques to my list of things that might tempt a thief.

There had to have been a serious amount of blood. Several hours after the fact, the scent remains strong. It permeates the ground, the stain extending beyond the outline of the deceased in what appears to be spray paint. Chalk would not have been adequate for the tough field grass amid patches of dirt and twigs.

"We'll work inward from here, Harley."

"Damned first responders tromped all over everything anyway."

"Doing their job," *she reminds him.* "Now we'll do ours."

"They shouldn't have moved her, Parks. Any first-year rookie in an ambulance knows that."

"Not our circus, not our monkeys. At least they secured the area and marked around the body first. Let's get to work."

I watch as they open their cases and slip on gloves. I like that they've placed their equipment at the very edge of the barricaded area so as to contaminate as little as possible. No need to make a hash of the investigation at this point. Even though I'm not impressed with him, I think the younger investigator is right. There won't be much on the ground that hasn't already been scrambled by those who removed the body of the victim. "Heart shot, according to the preliminary report," *Parks murmurs, looking at the outline where the body had lain.* "And not a nice, neat hole."

It's fortunate for me that these humans like to talk among themselves as they work. A shot to the heart would account for the heavy bloodletting. And would require a certain amount of skill. Quite a bit, actually. Especially if it proves true that the weapon used was an antique. That might account for the hole that was not nice and neat.

It would take a cold-hearted fellow to shoot a female through the heart. But there is a definite surplus of cold-hearted humans who inhabit this world. On the other hand, it could have been a very hot-hearted one. Hmmm, a love affair gone wrong is still a theory worth exploring. It wouldn't be the first such occurrence, by any means. Movies are filled with passion-induced violence. The fact that I don't understand it, doesn't mean it isn't factual. I don't understand a lot of what humans do in their spare—and not so spare—time. Still, it's early days with much evidence to be studied. The humans will do it their way, I'll do it mine. I'm not familiar with the term reenactment *so I'll have to do a lot of listening and pondering to figure that one out.*

"That little stool isn't overturned," Harley notes. "I'd say she was standing behind that table rather than seated at it when she was shot."

"Could be. The lack of blood-splatter on the table could also support that theory." *The woman doesn't dispute the possibility nor does she jump to agree with it.* "Forensics will tell us a lot from the angle of the bullet's entry and exit."

"But not everything." *Interesting. It's as if he wants an argument with her.*

"Never everything," *Parks murmurs, focusing her attention*

on the objects sitting on the table. She glances at the still-upright stool before turning that piercing stare toward the woods in front of her. "The stool is a bit left of center of the table. The cup and spoon even more left of the stool. I anticipate the coroner will determine she was left-handed."

"So?"

"So, her body was a fraction to the left of the stool and the report stated she was face up."

I am way ahead of the tenderfoot on this one. When Parks turns her attention back to the objects on the table, I start my search of the area in front of the left side of the table. Everything is still supposition at this point, and has to be prefaced by a most likely but, if she was seated when approached, she likely stood up on the left side of the chair and if she fell straight back, the assailant—again likely—stood directly in front of her, therefore, also to the left side of the table. If there are footprints to be found, that's where I would expect to find them.

And there they are, planted in the soft soil and close to the scene of the crime. If these are, indeed, the footprints of the killer, our victim had no fear of his or her approach. There was no scrambling away from the table to escape. She got to her feet to … what? … greet him? question his presence? perhaps even quarrel with him? All good possibilities yet to be answered, but answer them I will.

And, why, you wonder, do I bother? There are times I wonder, as well. But then, my answer is just as likely to be 'why not?' Some crimes pull me in and others are of no interest. Gas station robbery, too easy. I don't bore myself with those even where death is the outcome. Two people argue, one ends up dead, open and shut.

This case looks interesting enough to be worth my while, so back to the evidence at hand. The prints look to be from some type of boot with a treaded sole. The size is not distinguishing and could belong to either a man or a woman. For now, I'll continue to think of the killer as male. So much easier than thinking in terms of his or her at every point. I can visualize these prints belonging to said guilty party for a couple of reasons. First, it looks as if the wearer rocked back on the heels at some point. When the weapon was swung up and into place? Second, the prints then come forward toward the table. To ensure the victim is indeed dead? Perhaps. And perhaps not.

Even as I study the prints, I keep one ear tuned to the conversation of the two investigators as it continues on the other side of the table. Nothing yet has been said of particular interest. I've heard little beyond the typical exchange of humans used to working with one another.

"You video while I bag and describe."

I glance up as a small sound of irritation catches my attention and find Harley scowling at Parks' words. I'm confident by now that he's the junior officer and deduce from his expression that he either doesn't like being given an assignment or doesn't like the assignment itself. He would, perhaps, rather be the person in front of the camera rather than behind, although I don't see any glory in it as Parks reminds him to keep the camera focused on the object rather than herself.

Parks begins with the rifle, as I would have done. It looks to be old, a relic, and she describes it that way. It may or may not be the murder weapon, but she doesn't speculate on that. If it does prove to be, the more interesting fact will be that it was left behind. Why? Because it can't be traced or because it can be traced to someone who's not the killer? A frame? Interesting possibility but mere—and more—speculation at this point. My guess would be that the murder weapon is far from the scene of the crime by now.

The next item, which she describes as a cup of beans, has a utensil still upright in it, indicating that enough of the contents remained to support the utensil. It seems the killer interrupted her morning meal. But—beans?—what a nasty way to start the day. The victim's last meal was a dreary one. I find that sad.

Parks bags one last item, a small lantern of sorts, and removes her gloves. "That's about it for here, Harley. All we're going to do now is cast a couple of these prints in front of the table."

He nods. "Where the killer stood."

I considered that a reasonable comment, but Parks comes back with an equally reasonable response. I don't find fault with her words, but her tone could've been less tart. "Until we have the coroner's report, I won't begin to guess the force or angle at which the bullet entered her body. Without that, I can't determine distance or trajectory. Despite your hypothesis of events, we have no facts. Your suppositions could prove to be accurate, I'll give you that. In fact, I suspect they are. On the other hand, the killer could have been a sniper hidden in any one of the trees surrounding us, waiting from the moment she woke up."

She completes the casting process in the heavy silence that falls on the heels of her comments. She has selected the two closest to the table. They are the clearest of the prints but I'm less certain they're the most telling in terms of a depiction of the crime. They will, in any case, serve the same purpose if a suspect can be linked.

The investigators repack their equipment bags without further conversation. With a last glance back, I follow them from the woods and wonder if I alone hear the softly uttered "bitch" from Harley as he trails behind Parks.

Despite Park's shrewd assessment, like Harley, I'm inclined to believe the killer approached on foot and stood right in front of his victim as he shot her. Unlike Harley, I took the time to look for and follow the prints as they first left the woods and approached the victim. The tread of the sole, the pattern of movement, all pressed into dirt and damp grass, is fixed in my mind. Every aspect can be retrieved from my well-developed memory, if needed, at a later date. Harley needs to learn to trust and act upon his instincts. If they prove wrong, so be it. At least he will have tried and remained true to himself. Lessons he'll learn with time. If he stays in the business, that is.

* * *

With his thoughts back at the fairground, Wolf took the scenic route to Rita's sprawling property near the college. They were more than a decade past any bitterness but neither were they one another's favorite person. He wondered sometimes how they'd stayed married as long as they had. If he were a different kind of person, he might wish they hadn't but he wasn't one to live in regret. And there was no reason to believe he would ever have found someone who was right for him. Some people didn't.

Stepping out of the truck, he walked around to the backyard where he knew he was most apt to find his ex on a Sunday morning. The gate to her garden area made just enough noise as he pushed it open. Rita glanced up and laid her book aside. She didn't look surprised to see him but, then, Rita was not one to display emotion. Emotions made wrinkles.

"Good morning, Wolf. Would you like coffee?"

"No, I'm good."

"Have a seat then, and I won't have to get up." Her smile was faint. "What brings you here? Not that you aren't welcome. You know you always are."

Oddly enough, as loveless as their marriage had been, he did know that. He took the seat she offered. "Les asked me to come by and, yes, he's fine," he added as he saw her tense up. They didn't get along well but Rita loved her brother. Wolf would give her that.

"That's good then." In true Rita fashion, she didn't question, she simply waited.

Damn, he hated what he had to tell her. The reenactment was her brainchild. She'd worked night and day to bring it to life. The historical society might own the event, but Rita had been the force of nature that made it happen, sometimes in spite of the stodgy group who'd liked the idea but not the gritty reality of the work involved.

Wolf didn't bother trying to soften the blow. Rita appreciated bluntness more than any woman he knew. "There's been a murder, somewhere between the fairgrounds and the Boundary. Les said it was one of the reenactors."

She closed her eyes for a moment. Looking at her sitting there, he acknowledged to himself that she was, to this day, still one of the most beautiful women he'd ever seen. And he was as unmoved by that beauty as ever. Even more, somehow her vibrant red hair—still natural— and creamy fair skin paled beside a quick memory of wheat-blonde hair and freckled cheeks that he suspected had experienced more use of plain bar soap than facial products with exclusive labeling.

When Rita opened her eyes, she fixed him with a piercing look. "Are you working with Les?"

He hesitated, not sure that Les had yet made the call. Or that he even would. "Not my jurisdiction," he reminded. "But I imagine I will be, yes."

"I'll call Les to make sure of that. I want you on it."

Not even his influential ex-wife could get past those jurisdictional barriers if her brother balked at the last minute but damned if she wouldn't try.

"Regardless, Les promised to keep me in the loop, at a minimum," he said. He didn't mention that this visit was the price of that. No one wanted to bring Rita bad news. Ever.

"I need it wrapped up fast and no negative publicity." She tapped a fingertip with light precision in the center of her forehead. He recognized it as one of her self-reminders not to frown. "I'll have to see how we can make use of this."

And this was the predictable point at which Les would expect Wolf's intervention as his part of their bargain. "I wouldn't try that, Rita." He held up a hand as she opened her mouth to argue. "Seriously." She closed it again and that surprised him. "This was a young woman, very attractive, and she was shot through the heart. There's no way you, or anyone else, can turn any aspect of that into a positive."

Her exhale was long and slow. "Yes, you're right. Again."

He didn't smile. She hated when he was right.

She tapped her forehead again, a sure sign her stress level was rising. Odd that he could look at her and feel an affection he'd rarely known during their marriage. Some thought her vain. She wasn't. Rita was a good person with a dread of growing old because growing old led to dying. And that—the very idea of her own death—terrified her.

"Does Grant know what's happened yet? He will, without a doubt, be a complete pain in the ass about this."

"Dean Edmunds is all up in it," Wolf said dryly.

"Well, I'm sure I'll hear from him soon, so I appreciate the heads up."

Wolf got to his feet, seeing the comment as his opportunity to escape.

"You'll keep me informed?"

He knew Les was going to expect that as well. The sheriff had a real affection for his sister. He just didn't like talking to her. "I will as much as I can. I promise. Try not to worry too much about it."

Wolf had his own worry to deal with it. The thought niggling at the back of his mind was how little some of the old-school tribal members liked the idea of this reenactment at their doorstep. They weren't a bunch of crazies but, as in any segment of society, there was one or two among them who were.

Halfway back to the fairgrounds, he got the call from his director. Les had kept his word. Wolf was reassigned to the murder of Maisy McGuire until further notice.

Chapter 4

I've gleaned a pile of info on this case by doing nothing more than keeping my eyes and ears open. None of it official, I admit. It's all hearsay, but from very credible sources, namely all manner of law enforcement who've swarmed the area and aren't opposed to talking out of school amongst themselves, gray cat notwithstanding.

Victim's name, Maisy McGuire. Age, twenty-six. Occupation, middle school history teacher. Hobby, historical reenactments, specifically the Civil War. It appeared she, along with her partner for whom the police are still looking at as a person of interest, was a Civil War aficionado. They were also considered to be what reenactors dub hard core authentic, which somehow explains the nasty looking cup of beans that appears to have been Ms. McGuire's final meal.

And that last, the hobby bit, led me to some fascinating history— no pun intended—on these reenactments. It seems there are tens or *even hundreds of thousands of people who like to act out events or periods of history. And not just in America. Nope, this appears to be a global preoccupation with experiencing things from the past. Even disagreeable things, like war and executions and witch hunts and other manner of unpleasantries.*

No one that I've overheard has offered an opinion on why this is so. It simply is. And the deceased, Ms. Maisy McGuire, was one of those people. Whether or not this pastime plays into her death remains to be seen. The time and place may have been pure happenstance. The choice of vintage weapon, a mere fluke. Then again, perhaps not.

When my information gathering became repetitious, I turned my attention to finding Kylah. Checking up on her, as it were. Interesting as murder is, she is also of interest. I sense something vulnerable beneath her persona of strength. It's a mystery that tugs at me as much as this dead person.

* * *

Wolf parked near the barns. He intended to do nothing more than touch base with Les. This was his weekend off duty and he'd planned an afternoon on the lake with a fishing pole and a six pack. His first inclination had been to cancel those plans but he'd reconsidered. Unless the sheriff needed him elsewhere, that fishing expedition could prove beneficial to the investigation.

As he stepped out of his truck, he glanced across at the horse trailer still parked where Grant had grudgingly allowed it to remain. It was in a premium location alongside the barn and adjacent to the enclosed equestrian center. Wolf didn't see anyone near the trailer, but Jake was emerging from the barn leading a nice-looking horse, already saddled, toward the arena. The saddle wasn't like anything Wolf had seen before and he'd seen plenty. It took him a moment to realize that, though not archaic, it was a replica of an antique. He was close enough to see that the leather was far from old and in excellent shape.

Curious, only curious he told himself, he followed the man and horse through the roll-up doors where he paused long enough to allow his eyes to adjust to the dimmer light within. Jake had stopped just inside, as well, and stood watching as Kylah cantered another horse in a straight line down the length of the oval arena.

The animal beneath her appeared larger than average, his strides easy but reaching. His coat gleamed, dark and sleek, but Wolf couldn't tell if he were seal brown or a true black. Regardless, he was magnificent, his movements elegant. Without warning, in one obscenely graceful moment, the animal's legs folded beneath him, and he fell and rolled to his side. Wolf's heart jumped, and he lunged forward to rescue the rider, knowing she might already be pinned beneath the horse's bulk.

Jake's free arm shot out to stop him, catching him hard across his chest. "Whoa, hero. She's fine."

It took a moment for the words to make it through Wolf's instinctive reaction. It took him a bit longer to appreciate the wiry strength in the cowboy's outthrust arm.

He watched as Kylah rolled to one side of the horse which had not moved since coming to rest in the dirt. Wolf pushed at Jake's arm. Whatever was wrong, she'd need help with that horse. Jake's arm didn't budge, and Wolf fought the urge to bring it down with a knifehand strike, knowing it would be an abuse of his training. The cowboy posed no threat. Instead, Wolf stepped back and around the obstacle he presented.

"She won't appreciate you going out there." More than

the words, the quiet certainty with which they were spoken made Wolf hesitate. He glanced at Jake, then back at the girl who sat cross-legged some distance apart, watching the animal. After a moment, she got to her feet. The horse remained supine. She backed a dozen or so steps away before stopping, never once taking her eyes from the horse. When she stopped again, she made a subtle gesture with her hand, and the horse rolled over and pushed up, every bit as graceful as when he'd dropped.

"I'll be damned," Wolf muttered. He wasn't usually this slow on the uptake but then he'd never experienced or cared to experience a reenactment. If a cavalry scene were involved, no doubt Kylah and this horse were going to be a part of that.

He ignored Jake's snort of amusement at his expense and watched as Kylah walked toward them with a long, steady stride. She held out the reins to Jake and took those of the sorrel he'd brought in to her.

"He worked well today," Jake commented.

Kylah ran one hand down the dark brown neck. "Very well. I think he's pretty much ready to go." She gave Wolf one long glance, then led the second horse back into the arena.

Wolf suspected he'd been dismissed, but he didn't plan on going anywhere. Not yet. He settled onto the bleachers and watched as she walked, trotted, then slow-loped circles to warm the horse's muscles.

A glimpse of movement in the seating below pulled his attention from her for a moment. Somehow, he wasn't surprised to see the gray cat winding his way upward.

He sensed when Kylah was nearing the end of the warm-up period. She gathered the reins with a light hand before leaning her shoulders forward, where as before, she'd sat with hips forward and back straight. This time in response to whatever subtle signal she gave, instead of a slow roll-over, this horse reared straight up, pawing toward the high domed ceiling. When those front hooves hit the ground hard in a full-on run, Wolf's heart thudded, even though he'd known to expect something.

The cat, which had reached the section where he was sitting, leapt to the space beside him. He sat on his haunches and turned his gaze to the arena below where Kylah had stopped her horse and sat motionless, the horse equally motionless beneath her.

* * *

Kylah had learned long ago to focus on the here and now. Soon after Marty's death, within days, to be more precise. It was that ability to disappear into her work that had saved her. If she hadn't learned to ground herself, to put toxic thoughts away for periods of time, she would never have made it through.

Despite Dean Edmunds brushing aside this morning's death as accidental, Kylah suspected it was anything but. Throughout the morning, activity around the fairground had both heated up and cooled down. The presence of investigators had faded into the background as reenactors swarmed in, jockeying for the best parking spots for their campers and RV's. Faded but not disappeared. But with a job to do, Kylah pushed thoughts of police officers and ambulances with red whirling lights aside.

The arena, at least, was quiet and cool and almost empty. There would be reenactors with horses but those were not stunt animals and would have to be proven gun safe. She was not a reenactor and her horses were trained far beyond remaining calm in the face of gunfire.

Dismounting, she leaned her face into her horse's neck, breathing in the clean warmth of him. She could feel the steady gaze from the bleachers but she didn't glance up, as if by ignoring the sexy-as-hell man who watched her, he wouldn't exist. Like the mouse in the Christmas tree. The thought made her smile with a memory. It had been their first Christmas. First together, ever, first as a married couple. Their courtship had been whirlwind fast.

She'd suspected the mouse had come in with the tree, even ridden with it on some truck loaded with spruce and driven miles on stretches of interstate from the mountains. The tiny creature was tucked into the branches, back pressed against the trunk, and it was the first time she'd understood the phrase *still as a mouse*. The little creature was motionless, with its eyes closed tight. She told Marty, "He thinks if he can't see me, then I can't see him." Marty had laughed and agreed. They'd managed to capture the frightened creature in a paper sack and turned it loose together at the edge of the little woods that backed their yard. Marty had put his arm around her in the chill night air and squeezed tight. She could close her eyes and see the woods, the stars glittering above, even smell his favorite aftershave. But no matter how much she tried, she could no longer recall the exact sound of his voice. That terrified her.

Shaking off the moment and the fear, she led the horse from the arena.

By the time she reached the roll-up door, Wolf Stockton was waiting for her, the gray cat at his heels. She acknowledged them both with a glance and forced herself to smile. Then forced herself not to growl, when he matched his longer stride to hers.

"How long have you been doing that?" It was the kind of question that most often came with interviews. She could have answered in her sleep.

"Which aspect? Riding? Since I was capable of climbing on a pony when my parents weren't watching. Stunt riding?" She paused, thinking. "Twelve or so, as soon as I was strong enough to put a stunt saddle on one of my dad's animals without help."

"Which I interpret to mean he didn't consider you old enough or he would have helped you."

"Not old enough. Not strong enough. Not skilled enough."

"You proved him wrong?"

She snorted. "No, I proved him right with a broken arm."

They walked in silence for a few minutes before he said, "But you got back on."

She stopped and looked at him. "Why are you here?"

If he was startled by her blunt question, he hid it well. "Well, first off we've got the issue of the cat to settle."

"No, we don't. He's not mine."

He glanced down at the cat, who had stopped when they stopped and waited on his haunches as they talked. "I don't think he agrees with you."

She rolled her eyes. "Okay, let's table the first issue. What's next?"

"I saved your life. That makes me responsible for you."

"I'm not Chinese, and I doubt you are either," she retorted, proving she'd heard the same proverb he had at some point in her life. "Besides, who was trying to kill me?"

"I'm not sure *you* weren't."

His voice had softened, lost its playfulness. Unexpected tears burned her eyes. She turned, tugging on the reins in her hands as a flash of anger swept her at his words. No one saw her cry. Not even Jake, although he saw a lot of the other messy aspects of her life.

She didn't lose the man, or the cat, as she strode past, though she planned to rid herself of his presence the moment they reached the barn. Yes, she found him startlingly attractive, something she hadn't let herself notice in men in a long time. The fact that she'd noticed this man was more alarming than it was welcome. Still, he wasn't welcome in her life.

She stepped onto the gravel drive between the barns and the covered arena, then heard the roar of an engine and tires sliding on rock. In the same moment, she felt Wolf pushing her behind him. Her first frantic thought was the safety of her horse, and she leaned her body into the muscles of his shoulder to keep him from moving forward into the path of the vehicle.

Rocks spewed out from under the oversized tire closest to her, and she felt a sharp sting on her cheekbone. Her gasp drew a quick look and a hard curse from Wolf. She didn't need to raise her hand to her face to know there was a trickle of blood.

The young woman who opened the door and flung herself from behind the wheel of the truck stumbled as she whirled, scanning the jumble of vehicles around her. Her frantic gaze fell on Kylah and Wolf. "The sheriff! I was told he was here!"

Wolf pulled his cell phone from his pocket. "I'll get

him. Is someone hurt? Do you need an ambulance?"

"I don't know what I need." Her words came out in harsh gasps. "I don't know what's happened. I need to find Maisy! There's a barricade at our camp." Tears leaked from her eyes.

Kylah's heart sank. Maisy McGuire was the murder victim, and this woman was somehow connected to her. Beside her, she could hear Wolf talking to the sheriff.

Wolf put away his phone. "The sheriff is close and on his way." He looked at Kylah. "Could we all step into your trailer?"

So much for getting rid of him, she thought, handing her horse off to Jake who waited at the barn entrance. She led the way to her living quarters and didn't even sigh as the gray cat followed them in. Her life seemed to have taken a very weird turn, and she wasn't sure how much to blame on pure happenstance and how much to lay at her own door.

As they waited for the sheriff, she started the coffeemaker. Neither new nor fancy, it made the best coffee. She wasn't surprised when Wolf took his black and unsweetened. Their eyes met as she handed him a cup, and she saw his discomfort with the situation they shared, knowing the young woman's friend was dead and not knowing if they should be the ones to tell her. So, they hadn't.

Her name was Ella, she'd told them, Ella Necaise. After that she'd fallen silent, twisting and untwisting the plain copper bracelet on her wrist. Even seated, she was tall, with dark hair and uneven features that were more attractive than they should have been, particularly given the fact that her face was bare of any type of makeup. She declined Kylah's offer of coffee with a quick shake of her head.

Because it was too painful to watch her, Kylah focused on the gray cat who had made himself comfortable on the small steps that led up to her sleeping area. He met her look without blinking until a sharp rap on the door heralded the sheriff's arrival.

Opening the door, Kylah stepped over to sit beside the cat on the steps, and the sheriff took her spot, leaning against the counter of the kitchenette. He looked from Kylah to Wolf to Ella, then back to Kylah.

"What happened to you?" he barked.

She raised a hand to her cheek where his gaze had landed. She'd forgotten about the cut. "A rock. It was an accident."

He stared a moment more, then looked at Ella, who was staring at the cut on Kylah's face, "You knew Maisy McGuire?"

The blood drained from the other woman's face, leaving her sickly white. The sheriff's tone had been quiet and not unkind, but Kylah wished he'd chosen his words more carefully. Ella's eyes filled with pain. "What happened to her? What happened to Maisy?"

"I'm sorry," he said, sounding sincere. "She was murdered." And for that, Kylah knew, there was no easy way to convey.

Ella shook her head dazedly. She closed her eyes for a brief moment as tears seeped from beneath her lashes. "I don't believe you. I don't! No one would hurt Maisy." With a shuddering breath, she looked from one to the other of them.

"Do you know her family? We haven't been able to

contact anyone. We need someone to confirm her identity."

"Her family disowned her years ago. Me and Maisy … we're partners."

Kylah caught on quicker than either Wolf or the sheriff. Not working partners, although perhaps that, too. Life partners. Best friends and more. She sighed, feeling a familiar weight of sadness.

Ella got to her feet. "I'll go with you. I'll–" Her voice cracked and stopped.

As she stood facing the sheriff, he asked, "When was the last time you saw Ms. McGuire?"

Ella's head dropped. "Last night. Late. We had a stupid argument over something that never mattered anyway. I slept in my truck at a rest stop and came back to apologize."

The sheriff put his hat back on his head. "After we go to the …" He stopped. "Later we can go by my office and you can help with some questions."

"Yes. Of course." She looked numb.

As the door closed behind them, Wolf looked across at Kylah. "I think Ms. Necaise just became a suspect."

Chapter 5

I really need to show Mr. Wolf Stockton those footprints if they haven't already been obliterated through lackadaisical management of the crime scene. If I were in charge, much more of that area would have been cordoned off. Not that the crime scene investigators broke protocol—they didn't—they met all the minimum requirements I've learned from episodes of the Forensic Files show Dax and I watch. But I have to stress that minimum isn't always enough.

I can, and do, hope the prints are still at least somewhat intact. But how I accomplish getting Wolf to accompany me could prove tricky. He may be much more interested in remaining here to chat up the stunt lady. I'll have to be at my most persuasive.

Like Wolf, I believe Ms. Ella is now a suspect, at least as far as the law is concerned. And her size doesn't rule her out when matched with my recall of the prints in the soft soil of the hollow *where the victim was found. She's statuesque, not dainty, with a solid foundation in those lace-up boots she wore. It's unfortunate those lace-ups have left no discernable tracks in the gravel of the road here, no treads I can capture mentally to use for comparison of the treads in the soft dirt.*

It takes me more than a moment to get Wolf away from Kylah and moving in the right direction. At his insistence, she washed the cut caused by the rock and applied some sort of antiseptic before opening the door with the comment that she has work still to do.

Sure enough, Jake waits for her exit with yet another saddled horse. It's clear to me that he knows her well enough to discern her next move will be back to work.

A growl and a nip or two at denim clad legs and a resolute circling of some comfortable looking boots that didn't come from any bargain store and I'm satisfied to have Wolf following at my heels.

* * *

Wolf felt ridiculous. There was no other word for it. He was following a cat through the line of trees beyond the last scattered outbuildings. Even with that feeling, there was also little doubt in Wolf's mind that the cat had herded him with deliberate intent.

As curious as he was, his mind was still halfway back with Kylah West. She intrigued him even as he reminded himself that her life wasn't here and she'd be gone within a week or two. He also reminded himself that, except for an occasional one-night stand with a woman who didn't want anything more than that, his own life worked far better without a woman in it.

He gathered his thoughts back to the cat in front of him as they broke through a stand of trees at the base of a small hill. The first thing he saw was the barricade tape, fluttering in the soft breeze. The second thing was one of the sheriff's deputies glaring at his approach.

Recognizing Wolf, the other man relaxed. "Stockton. What the hell you doing out here?"

Might as well be honest. "Following the cat."

"Huh?"

"He pretty much herded me in this direction. Wouldn't take no for an answer." See, Wolf told himself. Ridiculous. The whole thing.

The deputy gave him a blank look, probably suspecting a joke. "Sheriff bringing you in on this?"

"Seems so. Thought I might as well take a look around while the area is secure."

He watched as the cat gave the deputy a dismissive glance then circled him and the barricade to the other side. Wolf was given one backwards glance and a chastising yowl. He shrugged at the deputy and followed the cat a short distance away, stopping where the cat stopped. He glanced down. "So far, you are a significant amount of trouble."

The cat grumbled a purr, then sat. He looked up at Wolf then down at the ground in front of him. When Wolf made a move forward, he hissed, and Wolf took a backward step, taking a closer look at the ground. At their obvious scrutiny, the deputy joined them, studying the faint prints along with Wolf. "Could belong to anyone. Dozens of reenactors already wandering these grounds."

"Yep." Wolf pulled out his cell phone.

"I'm sure the crime scene techies or whatever they call themselves these days took pictures."

"Yep." Wolf took several stills of the prints, then

made a video of their approach to the barricaded area, including two disturbed spaces side by side within inches of the table. It looked as if casts had been made. He hadn't missed the paint outline of the deceased behind that table. It would appear the forensics experts deduced the killer had stood there but at what point? As he pulled the trigger? Afterward, as he approached his victim? Wolf knew he needed to review the crime scene report as fast as Sheriff Mitchell could get his hands on it.

Wolf wandered the exterior of the barricade, taking several more shots of footprints. None were as defined as the first set which appeared to be made while the ground was still damp with morning dew. And none but the first set had drawn the cat's interest. Wolf didn't like where his mind was going with that thought.

He stepped back to take a panoramic scan of those prints before he slid his phone away and looked down at the cat. "Come on, cat." He needed to ask someone his name. He couldn't keep calling him *cat* if he was going to hang around. And Wolf had a feeling he wasn't going to go away.

* * *

I appreciate a cooperative human, especially one with the good sense to follow my lead. It doesn't always happen that way, and I never take it for granted. As we make our way back to the fairground proper, Wolf gives me a look. "Well, what's it to be? I'm headed for the lake and fishing. Are you going with me or staying here?"

Hmmm. This doesn't require a lot of thought. It's been a busy morning but has to be nearing the middle of the day and more than time for a meal. I doubt Kylah has anything of interest to me in that home on wheels of hers. Besides, I believe it would be of benefit for me to hang out a while longer with this Wolf person. I gathered from his exchange with the deputy guarding the crime scene, that he is, indeed, a lawman with ties to the murder investigation. Now that he and I have established a relationship, he could be a good source of information for me. Beyond that, a fishing expedition could provide the enticing possibility of a nice fish fillet. I liked mine cooked lightly, just until it flakes from the bone.

I'll return by dark to resume lending Kylah my presence—at least until this murder is solved. I don't think she's in any danger from either the killer or her own reckless behavior. Last night seems an aberration in her typical day. But her living quarters do seem a cozy place for me to hang while Dax is working.

And speak of the devil … not that he is, a devil, I mean … that's another of the many odd things that humans say. A short distance in front of us, Dax is with a very tall, dark-skinned man who is listening with interest as Dax talks in that soft voice of his. Most people do. Dax has that effect on people. I suspect it's his military background, which is as much a part of him as his army boots.

Intent on their exchange … likely discussing how to save all of mankind by their expressions … they don't notice us at first. But, no, that's not the case. The topic of their discussion is the weather, at least in regard as to how the possibility of rain could impact the placement of equipment and supplies. I gleaned from earlier conversation that moving things from one place to another with heavy equipment is Dax's primary responsibility while we're here.

When the dark-skinned man gives a nod and walks away, Dax turns to go, but stops when he sees us. He gives me a smile, "Hey, Callahan."

I notice the look Wolf gives me at the word but pay little attention as they exchange names and pleasantries as humans tend to do. Dax's stint in the military. Wolf's service with the Marshals. Interesting how these law enforcement types seem to mesh. My patience is long but not limitless. Fortunately, both soon recall they have things that need doing.

* * *

Wolf called Logan Yates on his way to the boat launch. If anyone had their finger on a pulse of possible unrest on the Boundary—about the pending arrival of a hoard of reenactors or for any other reason—it would be his best friend.

Logan, always up for fishing on a Sunday afternoon, met him at the marina, which was a pretty fancy name for the long, low framed building that housed a small diner and bait shop. The lake more than made up for that manmade homeliness with a fringe of leafy trees on grassy banks. In places, the roots of the trees were visible above the nearby water line, an intricate network of dark brown against the vivid green of the grass.

Logan's Native blood was more predominant than Wolf's but his looks showed it less. His hair was lighter, more brown than black and his eyes were hazel. Wolf had started ragging Logan about being a pretty boy when they hit their teens and the girls started chasing him. Wolf had gotten himself caught. Logan never had, at least not where a ring and ceremony were involved.

They shook hands once, hard, in their typical greeting and Logan's eyes dropped to the feline trailing him. "Yours?"

Wolf followed his glance. "Not long term. He kinda latched onto me last night in town." He didn't mention the stunt rider who'd also latched onto him and said, *you can take me home.* Or the fact that he'd been blindsided by an unexpected attraction that hadn't receded.

Before hitting the lake, they grabbed hamburgers—including one for the cat—along with fries and a couple of beers and sat at one of the outside tables. The weather was too good to be inside.

They ate in silence until Logan asked, "What's up?"

Wolf grunted then asked, "What gave it away?"

Logan snorted a laugh. "Thirty or so years of friendship?"

"How does the Boundary feel about this reenactment?"

Logan took another bite of his hamburger, watching the juice drip from his fingers onto his plate. His expression was one of sheer appreciation, but Wolf wasn't fooled. Logan wasn't thinking about the food in front of him, much as he might be enjoying it.

"The Boundary? As in the creeks and the hills and the meeting place?"

"Don't give me that ethereal bullshit. How do the people feel about it?"

"If you came around more, you'd know."

"I'm there every damned day," Wolf said without heat. This was an old *almost* argument. They'd get through it and move on.

"You *work* there every damned day," Logan clarified.

"You live off the Boundary, too."

Wolf's reminder had its usual non-effect on Logan. "But I do more than work there. I play. I visit the old people. I talk with the young people."

"I work with young people every day. I just don't happen to limit it to my people." And … the Eastern Band

… they *were* his people. Logan knew it, and that was why there was no heat in their exchange.

"What you do with the teens is a good thing, Waya." The use of his Cherokee name was as affectionate as it was intentional. "Too many would end up dead by their own hands if it weren't for people who give them hope. People like you." With that acknowledgement, Logan abandoned their wordplay. "So, what are you worried about with this reenactment?"

"Any disquiet? Any frustration? Or anger?"

Logan finished his hamburger and wiped his hands on a paper napkin. "Bound to be a little," he admitted. "The old folks are grumbling, but they grumble about something all the time. The kids are excited. A parent or two may be worried their young person will see a better life than what they have here." He crossed his arms on the rough wooden planks of the table and leaned forward. His eyes narrowed. "Someone made some mischief already."

Wolf finished his first beer and set the bottle on the table with a thump. "Worse than mischief. A woman was murdered this morning."

Wolf wasn't surprised that the word that came out of Logan's mouth was uglier than anything he'd heard his friend utter since their college days. "Is the law looking our way?"

"Not for now, but …"

"But it's inevitable, right?" Logan looked more resigned than angry, but there was anger, too.

"I think Les will look in every direction. Don't you?"

Logan sighed. "Yeah. Sheriff Mitchell's nothing if not thorough. And a prick."

Wolf couldn't help the snort of laughter that escaped

him. Les *was* a prick. Always had been. But he was good at his job, and they both knew it. So, there was little doubt, unless Maisy McGuire's partner confessed, the sheriff would turn his eye toward the Cherokee at some point during the investigation. Since Wolf had a gut-deep feeling Ella Necaise wasn't guilty, he didn't think that confession was going to happen.

"To answer your unspoken question, then, no, not everyone is thrilled with the idea of a reenactment. On the other hand, I haven't heard of anyone disturbed enough to kill to keep it from happening. If this woman's death would even do that."

"Keep the whole event from taking place?" Wolf gave that a moment's thought then shook his head. "Not from what I know. She seems to be ... to have been ... one of a thousand or so people who like to get involved with these things. Not an organizer or anything like Rita. Or Grant and Audra." He hadn't brought up Audra's name on purpose, but he couldn't help the quick glance at Logan's face as he said it. He'd always suspected Audra was the reason none of the girls chasing Logan had ever caught him. And Audra had ended up married to Grant Edmunds. Who was more of a prick than the sheriff ever thought about being. So, go figure.

Logan's gaze flickered to Wolf's, but his expression didn't change. "Any suspects?"

"Les thinks he's got one. She and her girlfriend had a fight. Girlfriend took off and slept in her truck at a rest stop. I think he's going to come up cold on it, but we'll see."

Logan tossed a crumpled napkin on the rest of his fries and stood. "Let's fish."

Wolf wasn't even surprised when the cat joined them as the boat slid into the water. The feline leaped to the bow of the boat, then curled up in the mate's seat, leaving Logan to sit where he could find a place after he'd pulled the truck and boat trailer to a parking area. Wolf chuckled at the look on his friend's face and started the engine.

* * *

I suppose I could choose to be irritated, maybe even insulted. The fishing expedition was a blinding success, and it was pleasant to see two men who found real pleasure in the art of the catch. At the end of the day, however, my man Wolf waived all rights to his share of the haul. I'm somewhat placated when I gather that the booty will be used by Logan to help a needy family. It seems the Cherokee take care of their own, unlike some of the unfortunate places I've visited where the wealthy walk past the unfortunate without a hint of compassion. Still and all, a meal of fresh fish cooked in butter would've made a decent afternoon treat.

"Why don't you come back to Ed's with me?"

From the sideways glance that accompanied the question, I deduce Logan already knows Wolf will decline. And that is exactly what happens.

"You know as well as I do that my uncle would let his wife and young'uns starve before he'd take anything from me."

"He's got a lot of pride."

"Don't we all."

And that's about all I learn from that exchange. Another mystery but not one that figures into solving the crime of the hour. I will, therefore, relegate it to a backburner, so to speak. And from what I gathered both now and during their conversation over hamburgers—

mine wasn't at all bad—a visit to the Cherokee land trust isn't going to happen soon. Logan doesn't see a real threat from that quarter which is fair enough. Beyond that, I doubt Wolf will invite me to tag along when he's on the job and seems to have reasons of his own for not being on the Boundary when he's off duty. Family reasons, I suspect. Human families can be so difficult.

Regardless, a lack of invitation won't stop me from getting where I need to be when I decide I need to be there.

Chapter 6

Jake brought a sandwich and thermos of coffee with the last horse. He handed Kylah the small canvas tote but held onto the reins.

She forced a smile as she saw the hint of worry in his eyes. "I'm not hungry." But she opened the tote and pulled out the thermos. The coffee was welcome.

"You're not hungry, because you can't handle drink worth a damn. You need to eat, K.T. Hungry or not. These horses deserve your best."

That stung, but she bit back a retort. Jake was right. Her work was off this morning. She'd been riding with technical skill but no heart. Her horses deserved better and so did Jake.

He kept an eagle eye on her as she unwrapped the

napkin around the sandwich. "It's time to get over it, Kylah."

Kylah looked up, startled. Jake didn't often call her Kylah and was irritated as heck when he did. His blue eyes were rock hard with more than irritation. "I am over it, Jake," she protested. "You know, I am."

"No. No, you're not. You've accepted his death. You're not over what he did and how he did it. Somewhere deep inside, you think he should've turned to you. You think you could've saved him, that somehow you *should* have. That's why you get drunk the same day every year and have for the last four years."

Without tasting it, she started eating the sandwich he'd brought her, that he'd fixed for her because he cared, really cared about what happened to her. Not because she was his livelihood, but because they'd saved each other four years back. Just as Wolf had done last night, Jake had made sure she reached home unharmed after she'd gotten herself shit-faced on the first anniversary of Marty's death. The anniversary of his suicide. The day the pain inside of him had become greater than the love he felt for her.

She'd been on the road then, too. When she'd stepped out of her living quarters the next morning, there he'd sat sprawled in a folding chair holding a thermos of coffee. Waiting for her to come out. They'd been together ever since. They were family.

"The first couple years, yeah. But not this year, Jake. Not even last year."

He took a sip of his own coffee, watching her with that calm way he had. He never questioned. Anything he knew about her she had shared when she was ready.

"Last year I was running from the fact that I was finally, truly angry at him. And it felt wrong. He's dead and I'm alive and 364 days a year I'm pretty much content, sometimes even happy. I got over the anger."

She started eating again, finishing her sandwich, realizing she was hungry now that she had something in front of her.

When she fell silent, Jake gave his attention to her horse and a last-minute check of straps and buckles. He always did that. Every time she rode. He never expressed worry or fear that something would happen to her, but he did his damnedest to make sure it wouldn't happen because he'd neglected something. The realization never failed to touch her.

Putting the lid back on the thermos, she got to her feet and took the reins from his hands. He studied her with affection, and she matched him look for look then took a deep breath. "This year I realized I can't recall the sound of his voice, of his laughter." Marty was always laughing, always a clown. It was what had first drawn her to him. And not once had she heard the pain hidden behind the façade of that laughter. "I'm losing him all over again, Jake."

"Then let him go. It's time." Jake took the tote from her and turned away, walking back toward the barn and the horses where there was always something that needed doing.

"I know," she said softly. "I know it's time, but I'd rather be angry at Marty than forget him altogether." Jake was too far away to hear her, but she wasn't talking to him anyway.

What she hadn't told Jake was that she'd also come to understand that Marty was never going to grow up and, if he hadn't died when he had, she suspected her love for him would have. And she didn't want to keep living on the memory of his love. She'd realized it was time to move on when she'd dressed and gone out on the town. Every other year, she drank alone, sitting in solitude in a dark corner of some bar. Last night, for the first time, she hadn't wanted to be alone. And all it had gotten her was a hangover, a gray cat, and a stranger who doubtless thought she was a good-time party girl. Not that it mattered what he thought. She doubted she'd ever see him again. Besides, she was better off alone. Just her and Jake.

* * *

The deputies made one last round as Jake and Kylah sat outside the trailer in companionable silence, watching the setting sun deliver a breathtaking show of colors across the top of the hills. She was in no hurry to return to the hotel room.

The officer who stepped out of the patrol car looked to be the youngest of the deputies Kylah had spoken to that day. His partner remained behind the wheel. Kylah saw his lips moving but couldn't tell if he was singing along to the radio or talking handsfree on his cell phone. She supposed one scenario as probable as the other.

"Good evening, folks."

Kylah thought the deputy looked a bit like a very young Barney Fife. She let Jake respond, which he kept to a tip of his cowboy hat.

"We're pretty much wrapped up here. We believe we've ID'd the culprit, but keep your eyes open and call if you see anything that concerns you or if you remember anything that didn't seem important at the time."

"So, you think it's *case closed*?" Jake eyed him curiously.

The deputy turned cautious, realizing his indiscretion. "Well, not quite but there was a quarrel not long before the crime was committed. Sheriff Mitchell thinks it's pretty cut and dried at this point."

Kylah recalled the shock and grief in Ella Necaise's eyes and very much doubted they had the guilty party identified, but she kept her thoughts to herself.

"We'll do that. And thank you for stopping by." Jake touched the brim of his hat.

"Well, just wanted to check on you folks. Y'all have a good evening."

He climbed back in the patrol car, and they watched as the tail lights faded.

"You think they're wrong." Jake's voice was quiet.

"So do you," she challenged. "You saw what I saw. The shock. And the grief."

"People can fool you," he said.

"You forget whose daughter I am. I've seen the world's greatest actors and actresses on the most acclaimed stages and sound sets. I'm hard to fool." She hesitated, then added, "As long as my emotions aren't involved." As they had been with Marty. Because she'd loved him, she'd seen what he wanted her to see.

Jake would never point that out to her but, then, he didn't have to. She got to her feet. "I'll see you in the morning."

"'Night, K.T."

* * *

Kylah turned onto the street leading to her hotel and realized her thoughts had turned to dinner, which surprised her. Hunger wasn't one of her strong points. She ate because it was necessary.

Regardless, the idea of sitting on her bed with an apple, studying her notes for the upcoming battle scenes, was unappealing. She felt restless. But the thought of being in a restaurant alone was also unappealing. Even so, a change might do her good. She could take her notes. Still study. She'd see if that idea held appeal after a quick shower.

She slipped on the backpack with her laptop and camera before she grabbed her purse. Stepping out of the truck, she closed the door then clicked the lock button on the ignition key. Halfway up the sidewalk to the entrance of the hotel, she caught sight of a man propped against the front of a truck and her steps slowed. As a course of habit, her hands were free with her purse turned for easy access to her concealed pistol. She didn't like over-reacting but there had just been a murder in this scenic little college town.

The man had his elbows behind him, leaning on the hood. A casual enough stance but not until she caught sight of the gray cat, almost invisible in the dark, did her shoulders relax. But instead of slowing down, her pulse seemed to speed up a bit. She'd think about that later, she decided.

She realized he was watching her, had been watching her since she pulled into the hotel parking area. She angled her path away from the hotel entrance and walked straight over to his truck.

"Hi." She felt awkward but it would have been more awkward to ignore him. He'd done her a solid favor getting her back to her hotel room in one piece, even if she hadn't asked for it. Or had she? The possibility was humiliating.

What a mess she'd made of things.

"Hungry?"

She ignored the voice in her head telling her to say no. "Yes."

He walked around her and opened the passenger door. "Climb in."

She hesitated. "I smell like horses."

He smiled. "I smell like fish."

Some of the tension, some of the uncertainty left her. She didn't have to think of this as a date. Not when neither of them bothered to shower and change. They were two people caught up in strange circumstances.

The cat jumped in ahead of her, then leaped to the back seat. Her day had been filled with oddities, that cat being the least of them. Murder was the greatest. Somewhere in between was having a rock flung at her face from beneath the truck wheels of a suspected murderess.

"What are you hungry for?"

His voice was low and deep, but not gravely like Jake's and far from boisterous like Marty's had been. It was soothing. It appealed to her. She realized in the same instant that he was watching her, waiting for a response, and that she was staring at him.

She began tugging at the seatbelt. "I'm not picky."

Wolf started the truck, and she fought a moment's panic. She didn't go out to eat with men. Ever.

"Relax."

"I'm relaxed."

He laughed and the soft sound made something inside of her unclench.

During the short drive, she discovered that he did not smell like fish at all. He smelled like fresh air and sunshine.

He smelled like man. She, however, without a doubt still smelled like horses and dust and leather.

He parked curbside at a small restaurant and walked around to open the door on her side. She stepped out, thinking the place looked a bit fancier than what she would have preferred, and he smiled at her as if reading her thoughts. "They have a little courtyard on the side. We'll sit there with Callahan."

"Callahan?" Her gaze followed his to the cat who'd gotten out when he did.

He shrugged. "So I learned today."

The cat glanced upward at them before, tail swirling in the air, he walked over to the intricate iron fence that separated an outside seating area from the sidewalk. After a look back, as if to tell them to hurry along, he stepped through to the other side.

"There's a lot more to him than a simple cat." Wolf held the door open for her.

Kylah shot him an amused look. "Animals are smarter than we are, by far, but I think that was a coincidence."

He placed his hand on the small of her back, and she fell silent, startled by the warmth that shot through her at his touch.

"You may change your mind about that coincidence thing," he murmured as they followed their hostess to a courtyard table. "I've had an interesting day."

Kylah wasn't sure of that change of mind but neither was she surprised when, once the hostess turned away, Callahan moved from the shadows to sit beneath their table. Watching them for cues was one thing—most animals did that—listening and reacting to their words was a very different thing.

Wolf waited until they'd placed their order with a waiter before he told her about visiting the murder scene with the gray cat.

"He *made* you follow him?"

She knew he could hear the skepticism in her voice, but it didn't seem to bother him.

"He convinced me to, that's for sure. It's tough to explain. He showed me some footprints that were outside the barricade." He did a decent job of describing the murder scene with its barricade, the roughly built table, and the outline of the victim. And the footprints beyond that.

"But the footprints could belong to anyone." She'd decided not to debate whether or not the cat had led him to those prints.

"That's what the deputy on the scene said, but Callahan—and I—disagree." He showed her the pictures and videos on his phone.

"These are pretty good shots," she murmured. "And some are nice, clear prints." But there was nothing outstanding about either the faint but visible tread or the size. "Looks like whoever they belong to walked out of the woods, stood square in front of the table for some period of time, before walking toward the victim then away, back into the woods."

"You've got a good eye."

"It's part of the training of choreography, seeing how things lay out … in your mind, on paper, then in action. Works the same in reverse, I guess. The difference is that this is on grass and sticks and dirt, not paper."

"Yeah, it's too bad it wasn't all dirt there. The prints would be a lot crisper. I hope the ones the crime scene workers casted will provide more information."

"The two deeper indentions?"

"Yeah. About all I can tell from the prints that were left is they were made by some kind of work or hunting boot."

"Which could belong to any of several hundred reenactors who have been scouring those slopes looking for the perfect location to set up their tent or their station." He had her curiosity stirred now. It intrigued her to know that he was looking at the prints through the eyes of a lawman. "Do you see anything else?"

"Just what I'd expect. Whoever wore those boots walked away from there a hell of a lot faster than he or she walked up."

"Which could mean they were guilty or they were frightened by what they stumbled upon."

"Too frightened to find help or call it in?"

"There is that," she agreed. They both knew that scenario was unlikely. She nodded her head toward the phone he'd laid on the table. "Did you share those with the sheriff?"

"Not yet. I asked him to meet me at the fairgrounds in the morning. I wanted to be at the scene when we looked at what I'd photographed. Unfortunately, the forecast calls for another good shower or two after midnight. There won't be much trace of any prints by morning. But maybe he can visualize in his mind what was there."

She smiled. "Like choreography."

He smiled back, and it occurred to her their conversation should be morbid considering the subject matter. Instead, it felt anything but that. Because they were being analytical, she told herself, not for any other reason.

She hesitated before asking, "What is your role in all of this? You're not just an interested bystander."

"Bystander, no. Interested, yes. Beyond that, I'm with the Cherokee Marshal Service."

He'd surprised Kylah yet again. She caught him watching her and knew he'd realized it. He looked chagrined as if he thought he'd made a mistake in not telling her his profession. She wanted to shrug and tell him not to worry about it, that they weren't likely to see each other again after tonight. As soon as it crossed her mind, she remembered how short a time ago she'd had that same thought and yet here he sat, right beside her. So much had happened in less than a single day. The realization left her exhausted. Or maybe it was the fact that she was running on too little sleep.

"So, you're a U.S. Marshal." She wasn't, she realized, the least surprised by the revelation.

"And you're a movie star's daughter." She stilled, but he said it idly, his gaze holding hers, and she could tell how little that fact meant to him.

"You did your homework."

He nodded. "You're Madeline Breck's daughter. She has a lot of fans around here."

She noticed he didn't say he was one of them. That was okay. She wasn't either. It was a happenstance of birth that she'd been born to one of the more acclaimed stars of recent decades and nothing she could, or wanted, to take credit for.

He reached across the table to take her hand and—in keeping with every other crazy thing going on around her—she let him.

Chapter 7

On the drive back to the hotel, Wolf made his admission. "Your man, Jake, kept me from making a fool of myself today." He forced his attention to the road but felt her watching him.

Her glance was curious. "Jake? How's that?"

"I didn't realize you were a trick rider."

"Well," she said, "I prefer the term stunt rider or horse trainer, but okay."

"When that horse dropped to the dirt with you in the middle of the arena, my heart dropped right along with him. I thought you were crushed."

"Ah. Sorry. It's supposed to be dramatic—for the audience—but I guess it can be a little much for someone trained in emergency response. Most lawmen are, right?"

"There's that, but it felt a little more personal for me." He wasn't sure why he admitted to that when he wasn't crazy about the fact that he even felt that way. He had a suspicion this woman was going to disrupt his well-ordered life.

"We've only known each other since this morning." He could sense her pushing the distance into place between them as he turned into the hotel drive.

"Since last night," he pushed right back.

"I'm not counting that, as I don't remember much of it," she admitted.

"I remember it."

She didn't answer, but he felt her gaze on his face.

He was careful to signal his intentions by pulling up to the front entrance of the hotel rather than parking the truck and walking her up to the side door. He didn't want things to turn awkward, didn't want her getting prickly on him. He suspected she could do that in an instant. He still couldn't believe she'd agreed to go with him, still felt a mild surprise that he'd asked her.

He liked that she waited in the truck for him to walk around and open her door, an indication she was confident enough in her independence not to feel threatened by a guy's preference to be a gentleman. Or maybe that was her movie star's daughter's upbringing.

She took his hand to step down, and he held onto hers until they reached the door, which slid open as they approached. He'd noticed earlier that her nails were pretty, filed short but polished with something that sparkled. She sparkled.

"Thank you for dinner," she said.

"Thank you for going with me." He watched as she and the cat went inside.

* * *

Wolf walked into the snug home he'd built for himself years ago, after letting Rita keep the too-large one they'd built together, the one she'd designed and loved far more than she'd ever loved him or any other person. He switched on a few lights and looked around, much less content than he'd been twenty-four hours earlier.

Damn.

After a hot shower, he pulled a beer from the fridge, then sat at the bar studying the photos he'd made of the crime scene that morning. Closing them out, he hesitated, then sent Kylah a text, wondering what she'd make of the fact that he was still thinking about her.

* * *

Kylah lay in the dark of her hotel room, thinking through the next day's drills for her horses, something she did most nights when she was this close to a performance. She heard a soft ding from her phone and raised it, illuminating the screen so that the text was visible. The two simple words: good night. The fact that he'd sent them curved her lips in a faint smile. She placed the phone back on the nightstand and rolled to her side, exhausted but unexpectedly content.

It was morning but still dark out when her phone dinged with another text, this one from Jake: I'm cooking.

She was smiling as she rolled out and headed for the shower. She and Jake were so predictable. Like an old married couple. From time to time someone would think that's what they were. Every now and again, she wondered what Jake wanted from his future, but she'd never felt more than friendship and a certain responsibility to him and for him. As far as she knew he had no family. There was an ex-wife somewhere, but she'd left him when he wouldn't leave rodeo. All he'd ever said was that it was his fault he'd loved the sport more than her. And the sport hadn't been faithful to him. Stomped one too many times by one too many bulls, he'd emerged from a hospital, broke, with a permanent limp and no way he knew to make a living except doing what he could no longer do.

For Kylah, he was as much friend and mentor as employee. He worked for room and board and what little cash he'd accept from her. The rest she put up in CDs in his name. He knew they existed. She showed him where they were in her office safe but he wouldn't touch them. She had no idea why.

* * *

Kylah could smell bacon frying as Callahan followed her out of her truck. Jake stood at the outdoor grill near the trailer, and the cat settled into one of the folding chairs that was a perpetual part of their lifestyle. The one closest to Jake and the food, she noticed.

"Morning, Jake. We've got a lot to do today."

He handed her a cup of coffee and grunted. "Well, whatever you got on your list, you can add one more thing. That Edmunds fellow called a meeting with the organizers, the staff they've hired to help, what he called unit commanders and their officers, and paid performers."

"Interesting. What time?"

"One o'clock. At the college."

Damn. That was right in the middle of her day. "Who

do you suppose are paid performers besides us?"

He cut her a glance. "Probably nobody. And that would be you, not us."

"Huh." She drank her coffee and waited for her bacon and eggs with as much anticipation as the cat.

* * *

I admit that meal was nothing to curl my nose at. Jake's handy with a skillet and spatula, almost as good as Dax. A little heavy on the pepper maybe, but Kylah doesn't seem to mind and this is her domain. I notice he watched like a hawk to make sure she didn't skimp. He didn't have any concerns on my account, just stood ready with second helpings of both eggs and bacon and was savvy enough to withhold the grits. Even with a generous covering of melted butter— the real thing from real cream—I find what is bits of ground corn as unappealing as grains of rice. Both are too bland for words and neither worth edging out beef or pork.

I recognize the sound of the well-tuned vehicle approaching. With Jake and Kylah both disappearing into the barn, I'm left to greet Wolf Stockton. There may be some disappointment in that for him, but he'll have to accept the hand he's dealt, and I won't take offense. I pretend not to notice his careful look around as he leans against the side of his truck at my approach. A man has to have his pride.

"Good morning, Callahan." *And he's a good man, at that. I appreciate being greeted by name.* "The sheriff will be here soon if you'd care to join us on a brief expedition back to the murder scene." *And a wise one, too, to recognize the value in my presence.*

The sheriff, on the other hand, doesn't give me so much as a look upon his arrival. I doubt he even notices my presence as we traipse back across the hills to the site of the murder. Like me, Wolf navigates the uneven terrain with little effort while the sheriff reveals his lack of fitness with a bit of huffing and puffing.

"This better be worth my time, Wolf."

"It may or may not be. Did the crime scene investigators show you pictures of footprints directly in front of where the victim was found?"

"No."

"Any of your deputies?"

"No."

"Then it should be worth your time."

The sheriff grunts his displeasure but I'm not certain if it's displeasure at Wolf's sarcasm or displeasure at the implied gap in the diligence of his deputies.

When we reach our destination, the tape forming the barricade sags between posts that lean in the rain-sodden ground. The sheriff stands in front of the table that has been left as found as he studies the photos and videos on Wolf's cell phone screen.

"You know these could belong to anyone?"

Well, he's heard that before. Twice.

"Your deputy pointed that out to me—while I was doing his job for him."

Touché. The sheriff's pained expression indicates a direct hit.

"Are you still looking at Ella Necaise?"

The sheriff walks to where the footprints would have been, were they not now washed away. He stands in silent contemplation in front of the somewhat crude-looking table. "No. There were security cameras at the rest stop and she chanced to park within range. She was there, asleep in her truck, at the time of death. So, unfortunately, she's cleared."

"But fortunate for her since you now know she's innocent," Wolf said dryly.

The sheriff ignores that but I'm pleased when he shares more information we need for our investigation. "The autopsy confirmed a heart shot from someone standing right in front of her. Fairly close up. Ten to twelve feet."

"So right about where you're standing now." *Just where I showed him the footprints that he documented. Wolf manages to keep his tone from saying* I told you so. *Pretty darn good of him. I'm not sure I could have done as well with that.*

"Yeah."

"So, the murderer stood right in front of that woman, looked her in the eye, and pulled the trigger. That's cold."

"Damned cold." *The sheriff looks more thoughtful than disgusted at the implication.*

"And she just stood there." *Wolf is pressing his point. I wonder if he doubts the good sheriff can get there on his own. As for me, I definitely have my doubts.*

The sheriff nods. "Which tells me either it happened fast or she didn't believe whoever did it would pull the trigger."

"So, you think it was someone she knew?" *It's clear Wolf already believes this to be the case. And so do I.*

"I'd say knew and trusted or at least had no reason to distrust."

We all three stand and stare at the ground where she fell, trying to picture what happened in that instant in time.

"And the other thing ..."

Wolf looks at the sheriff, expectantly, and so do I.

"Forensics has identified the murder weapon as the Burnside carbine that was found on the table. We're keeping a lid on that fact for now."

Wolf says nothing, but I see the speculative look and I get the gist of that information immediately, as has Wolf. Her murderer was not concerned that the rifle would be found along with the body, may even have wanted it to be identified as the murder weapon. That fact would indicate that the rifle could not, in any way, be tied back to him or her. The possibilities are endless and very, very interesting.

But even as that thought occurs, even as we stand here considering the implications, something tugs at my thoughts. I sense it's something important, though it escapes me for the moment. I'll have to ponder more on this later. Now, I have to get back to Kylah. I don't want to miss our meeting at the college.

As we retrace our steps, Wolf asks the question I wish I could voice. "Have you traced ownership?"

"I've got someone working that now. I'll talk to them as soon as I have a name." *I could almost hear Wolf thinking. Apparently, the sheriff could as well.* "I'll tag you when I know something, see if you want to sit in."

"I'll want to be there." *Wolf's response left no doubt of the fact.*

I glance up in time to see Sheriff Mitchell nod. "Afterward, you can give my sister an update. Something vague but reassuring." *Wolf makes that peculiar snorting noise humans use to indicate various negative emotions. The sheriff doesn't seem offended as he ignores the sound and asks a question instead.* "Anybody on the Boundary you think I need to be keeping an eye on?"

"You don't think this is going there, do you?" *Wolf sounds more exasperated than alarmed.*

"No." *I sense the sheriff is discouraged.* "I don't. But I've been wrong before, and nothing about this murder is making a lot of sense to me so far. I keep waiting for the other shoe to drop."

* * *

As irritated as she was by what she considered a

summons and one that disrupted her work with her horses, Kylah admired the beauty of the campus situated in its cove of stately trees. The custodians had allowed the grounds to be littered with leaves from the previous autumn; but, since that detritus was confined to a precise circle around each tree, it was clear the *natural* effect had been created and maintained with considerable care.

The sign at the front was dignified. College of the Carolinas, Albrecht Creek Campus. Plain black lettering on plain white background, but that background appeared to be a natural white stone, embedded in a slab of rock that had neither appeared by miracle nor transported itself to that precise curve in the drive. Money had been spent. Quantities of it.

Kylah parked and held the door open as the gray cat exited the truck with her. She hadn't bothered to change from denim and boots. She'd stepped down from a horse and into her truck, ignoring Jake's lifted brow. If Dean Edmunds didn't care for her attire, that was his discomfort not hers. She had more horses to ride after this meeting. Jake would let her know who needed settling with exercise and who needed a rest.

An impeccably dressed woman waited near the door as Kylah walked through the main entrance. The woman didn't bat an eye at her casual garb but stared at the cat who trotted along behind her. "Oh, I don't think …"

Kylah scooped Callahan up in her arms. "He's with me. Where does Dean Edmunds want to meet?"

She sighed and pointed to a hallway on her left. "There's a small auditorium there. The first set of double-doors on the left."

"Thank you." Kylah turned and followed the woman's

directions, stepping into a room that held more people than she'd expected to see. When she'd been contacted about performing in this event, she had studied up on reenactments and reenactors and decided it had a lot in common with a movie set. The major difference was that most reenactors, other than those commanding the units and some few who participated in more intricately staged scenes, weren't paid. She and Jake had come a week ahead of the actual event to give her horses time to acclimate and her time to scout over the places she would be expected to ride them. Their safety was her primary concern.

Glancing around, she decided she was in some kind of lecture hall and took a seat at one of the tables. So far, Callahan seemed content to sit in her lap but who knew how long that would last. He was a cat with a mind of his own.

She recognized Dean Edmunds, standing at the front of the room talking with an older gentleman. A woman stood at his side. Her hair and eyes were as dark as his were light, but where his skin was florid, hers was the peaches and cream variety of fair. She was, however, every bit as tall as he.

At one o'clock sharp—Kylah checked her phone— the dean started speaking. He had a voice that carried well through the room. Even seated near the back, she could hear him without straining.

"Thank you for coming and I'll take as little of your time as possible. I'm sure you're all as busy as I and my staff. For those of you who don't know me, I'm Dean Edmunds." His expression made clear he considered the introduction a nicety more than a necessity. "I'm head of the history program on this campus. My wife," he gestured toward the dark-haired woman beside him, "is director of our theatrical department." Kylah wondered if she imagined the slight sneer when he said the word theatrical. "We're both avid reenactors and are excited to be a part of this event, which has, in fact, been placed under our leadership."

He nodded and beamed at the scattering of applause.

"I'll give you a bit of history. For those who are unaware, the College of the Carolinas is a private, multi-campus college, one of the most prestigious in the country. This campus was recently gifted acreage near the Qualla Boundary."

No, she hadn't imagined the sneer. There it was again and stronger upon mention of the adjacent land held by the Eastern Band of Cherokee.

"The endowment includes the site of a Civil War battlefield. An unexpected but welcome discovery."

Another scattering of applause. Another self-satisfied smile from Grant.

"Our college board, with the full support of the town's historical society," he gestured toward a table at the front of the room, "opted to host the First Reenactment of the Battle of Albrecht Creek. Our purpose, of course, is the enlightenment of the students whose education has been entrusted to our care. War is a terrible evil and there are lessons to be learned, more so in a war where brother bore arms against brother. To that end, aspects of the reenactment, essays as well as active participation, have been included in this and future history and theatrical courses."

Halfway through that speech, Kylah transferred her attention to his wife, who remained at his side, quiet and without expression. Kylah didn't know many people, other than skilled actresses and actors, who could accomplish that appearance of not thinking and not feeling anything at all. But, then, it could be she excelled at it since she was at the head of the college's theatrical program.

Grant Edmunds, on the other hand, was not much of an actor. He just thought he was. Kylah saw when he changed expression from proud academic to concerned citizen, so she was prepared for his shift in topic.

"Some of you, by now, perhaps even all of you, are aware of the loss of one of our reenactors. Law enforcement is fully engaged in the investigation and we have no reason to feel there is a threat to any participant of this event. We do ask that you keep your discussions of the incident minimal and discreet." Kylah wondered if he meant himself and his wife or if that was a royal *we*, as in all of the college and law enforcement combined and under his helm. It wouldn't matter, of course, and it wouldn't be heeded. Gossip was gossip and murder was big gossip indeed, though Grant had neither called it murder nor acknowledged an actual death. It was a loss as if someone had misplaced a person, nothing more than an incident to him or, perhaps, he hoped that was all it would be to his audience.

A movement near the double-doored entrance which had been left open on one side caught Kylah's attention. Several young people filed into the room. Their clothing was casual but neat. Though their expressions were solemn, she caught a spark of excitement or nerves in some of the glances that swept the room. Students, she surmised, suspecting things were about to get interesting. The murmurs around her grew louder in tacit agreement with her suspicion.

Grant's wife touched his arm and whispered something to him. He turned and his face darkened at the disruption.

The girl who stepped forward looked of Asian descent to Kylah. She had beautiful dark eyes and arresting features. "Good afternoon, Dean Edmunds. The student body would like a voice at this meeting."

"Ms. Farraday, the student body was given full voice at several of the joint discussions between the college and the historical society."

"Our concerns were not heeded and now the violence that we feared has occurred."

"That investigation is in the hands of our very capable law enforcement."

"It's not the investigation we wish to address."

Kylah had to hand it to the girl, who stood without fidgeting or any other hint of nerves, despite the fact that Grant was doing his best to intimidate with drawn brows and a piercing glare. The small group of students with her tensed and shuffled their feet when he turned that look on each of them in turn. Not well-versed in identifying nationalities, Kylah nonetheless appreciated the diversity of the group in their appearances and demeanors.

Ms. Farraday outwitted Grant by the simple ploy of remaining silent after her brief response, forcing him to make the next move. After an awkward moment, he nodded. "Speak your piece."

The girl took two steps forward and focused her attention toward the table where the historical society had been seated.

"Good afternoon," she said again. "The student council here with me today represents the interests of the student body. Not every member agrees with the majority, but they stand for that majority nonetheless. We are opposed to violence. We are opposed to war. We are opposed to this reenactment which glorifies the violence of war. And now it has brought that violence to us, as feared. We feel unsafe. We ask that the society and the college terminate the reenactment that we opposed from the beginning."

Not one member of the historical society responded to her speech by so much as the blink of an eye. Several sat with crossed arms. Others leaned back against the hard seats of their chairs. One or two propped elbows on the table in front of them, as if bored. After a quick glance at her husband, whose features registered complete fury, Mrs. Edmunds spoke to him in another quiet aside before addressing the young woman. Her well-modulated tones carried well throughout the room.

"With respect to your position and representation of the student body, Ms. Farraday, the college does not agree that the reenactment glorifies war. Under the guidance of our very knowledgeable historical society," she gave a nod in their direction, "we've orchestrated the event so that it depicts the truth. There were no winners in the battle of Albrecht Creek, only losers. War has been an unpleasant reality throughout our history, the history of this nation. To ignore that fact is to live in ignorance. To live in ignorance is to invite repetition of the mistakes of our past. The loss of life of one of the reenactors is as regretted as it was unexpected, but we have no reason—at this point—to believe it bears a direct relationship to the event itself. Thank you for voicing your concerns. Please return to your classrooms at this time."

Kylah wasn't sure if it was a testament to their respect

for the woman who headed the drama department or to their acceptance that this last-ditch protest had been an exercise in futility, but Ms. Farraday nodded and signaled to the student council to follow her from the room. A young man with dark hair and thin, defined features stood closest to the door. He stepped back to let the others pass through the opening ahead of him. But Kylah realized that what she had taken for a polite gesture toward his classmates was something different when he took a step forward to glare at Grant.

"This is wrong, Dean Edmunds. You're vainglorious and you're pompous. Your pride comes at the expense of safety for the entire student body!"

"Mr. McDaniel!" The dean's tone was curt. "Wait for me in my office. I'll meet you there when this meeting is adjourned."

Personally, Kylah thought Mr. McDaniel had nailed the vainglory and pomposity. On the other hand, the student appeared to have enjoyed his moment of drama far too much for her to credit it with any kind of sincerity. She wondered if he were part of the theatrical group. His height and build seemed well suited for the football field but, more often than not in her experience, appearances were deceiving.

The young man spun on his heels and marched from the room with shoulders back and head held high. Kylah wouldn't have been that age again for any amount of money. Too much angst, too little autonomy.

Grant straightened his tie and jacket as if he'd been in actual fisticuffs. A little drama there, too, she thought.

When he resumed speaking, it was as if he'd never been interrupted.

"I'd like for you all to take the time to get to know one another and my ... ah, our," he smiled at his wife, "four assistants who are seated at the table next to the door. Your interaction and cooperation with each other and with them will be crucial in the coming days, and we have little time to be ready. I know all of you—in particular you unit commanders and officers—know your jobs and know them well. Your knowledge is key to our success. Our target audience, students from campuses around the country as well as your everyday history buffs, will be descending upon us in a few days. We're excited and hope you are as well. Tomorrow we'll have a dress rehearsal so be sure you and your teams are in costume and know your places. We'll be doing some staging, making last minute adjustments if needed. No actual acting. Don't overburden yourself with props because there will be a good bit of moving about, but be certain what you have with you is authentic."

Kylah made her exit when the mingling began. She'd find who she needed to talk to when she needed to talk with them, and she wouldn't fight a crowd to do that.

Callahan trotted right along behind her. He seemed no more impressed with the speech they'd endured than she was.

Chapter 8

Kylah ignored the slight lift of her spirit at the sight of Wolf's truck parked across from her trailer when she returned. She couldn't afford that kind of distraction. She didn't want it and wouldn't risk it.

She'd called Jake to let him know she was on her way back and would be ready for another horse. Seeing Wolf's truck at least prepared her to see him walk out of the barn beside Jake, who brought her next mount.

Taking the reins from Jake with a smile and thanks, she turned to Wolf, battling her own emotions. The smile she'd given Jake faded. "I would've thought you'd be on the job by now."

"I'm headed that way," he said without inflection, but his glance held a question.

Kylah led the horse away from them, feeling unsettled. It wasn't Wolf, but her reaction to him, that had rattled her. She paused to take a deep, cleansing breath before she mounted. This was the youngest and greenest of her horses, rescued from a kill pen by a friend who'd recognized something special in her but not the kind of something that lent itself to just any rider or any job. The young mare was playful and oh, so smart. Her progress had been steady, but she still needed lots of time and patience so Kylah gave her slow, quiet work they could both enjoy before she moved her on to the actual lesson.

When she heard Wolf's truck start, she knew her mind hadn't been as focused on the task at hand as it should have been. Normally sounds and activities around her faded when she worked. But she didn't lie to herself; she'd been listening. She told herself the quick jab of disappointment at his leaving was only because she knew she should have been less distant toward him, all things considered. She made sure she gave the mare the focus she deserved for the remainder of the workout. She'd think about Wolf and how he made her feel later.

* * *

"I sure didn't make Wolf feel welcome," she admitted to Jake as she brought the mare back to the barn. She didn't offer up the reins so he fell into step beside her. She could feel him searching her face, but he didn't say anything until they reached the mare's stall.

"You should cut yourself some slack, K.T."

She eased the bit from the mare's mouth and slipped her halter off. "I'm trying." She hesitated. "He's one of the good guys."

"So are you." He finished loosening the saddle and lifted it from the mare's back. "You're thinking he won't come back around because you can't sort your feelings?"

She picked up a brush, embarrassed with the whole conversation. This was Jake, for crying out loud. "Why would I care what he does and doesn't do?" Then, because this *was* Jake, "I don't know what I think."

"Seems to me you should stop thinking so much and start accepting how you feel."

"It's too soon for what I feel. It takes time to know someone."

Jake placed his calloused hand on top of hers to still the movement of the brush across the muscular flank. "How long did you know Marty before you married him."

"Two years." Her throat still ached when she thought of their fun and funny courtship.

"How well did you know him after those two years?" Jake lifted his hand from hers.

"I didn't know him at all," she whispered to herself. Jake already knew the answer to his question.

By the time she had finished brushing the mare, she realized she was on her own in the barn with the horses. Jake had given her his bit of wisdom and left her alone with it. The words she muttered as she fastened the stall door were not words of appreciation, even though she suspected he was more right than wrong.

She tapped on the door to the living quarters to let Jake know she was headed out. The gray cat was not in evidence. On the drive back to the hotel, she considered dinner options. She knew better than to skip meals, but she couldn't think of anything she wanted delivered or any place she wanted to go.

Her room was pretty much as she left it, neat because she couldn't stand chaos, with clothes folded and stacked for easy access each morning. But the bed was made and the bath linen had been replaced.

Jake would be feeding horses in another hour. She could suggest he drive into town, and they could toss a coin over picking a restaurant. It wouldn't be the first time. She dug deep in her purse and found her phone. After staring at the blank screen, she typed a one-word text she had no intention of sending. Then she hit send. Tossing the phone to the bed, she turned on the shower and stripped, letting steam fill the room as hot water sluiced over her head and shoulders.

As she stepped out of the bathroom, one towel wrapped around her body and another wrapped around her wet hair, the screen on her phone lit up. Right below her **Hungry?** was **Yep** Smiling, she combed out her hair and used the hotel hair dryer to get it halfway there. Clean jeans and a loose-fitting top and she was done.

* * *

Wolf watched as Kylah walked toward his truck. She'd surprised him. He glanced at the cat who occupied the passenger seat. "You gonna let her have that spot?"

Callahan stretched as she opened the door and shifted his fur and muscles to the console before making a light leap to the back seat.

"Hi." The word was soft. Sexy.

"Hi, yourself." He watched as she slid into the space the cat had vacated. "Where do you want to eat?"

She pulled her seatbelt and clicked it into place, then gave him a smile. "You pick. Jake says I need to quit thinking so much so there's no telling where we'd end up if I have to decide."

"You always listen to Jake?"

Her smile turned to a grin. "I don't do anything *always*, but when I'm being wise, yeah, I listen to Jake."

He returned the grin and pulled out of the parking spot. He could feel the difference in her as he headed toward one of his favorite places on the outskirts of town, a little bar and grill with good country music and steak cooked right, no matter how you liked it. He wasn't sure what the difference was, but it was there. A lightness he hadn't sensed the previous evening.

When the truck stopped, Kylah placed a hand on his arm. "Do you want your apology now or over dinner? I was barely civil earlier, and I'm sorry for that."

Before he could think too much, like Jake accused her of doing, Wolf leaned in and brushed her cheek with his fingertips. He would've liked to turn that touch into a hell of a lot more. But here and now wasn't the place or the time. He shifted back in his seat, the better to see her eyes. "Apology not needed or it's accepted or whatever you prefer."

She studied him in silence, and he didn't have a clue what was going on in her head. But, with that, the three of them got out of the truck and headed for the entrance, Callahan taking the lead. A waitress motioned them toward a table, then followed with two glasses of water and her order pad.

Like Kylah, Wolf ordered the rib-eye then looked the waitress in the eye. "There's a cat under the table."

"Hon, I saw him when y'all came in. He would've been hard to miss. How does he like his steak?"

"Medium rare with the excess fat trimmed."

"I'll be right back with your drinks and a bowl of water." With a wink for them, she closed her order pad and walked away.

Kylah lifted her brow at Wolf.

"What? We've been hanging together, you know. He prefers fish but I wanted a steak."

"And you learned this in two days?"

"It's been a busy two days and a guy's gotta eat." But, for tonight, Wolf was determined to not talk about murder. "I could get used to having dinner with you every night."

She'd glanced toward the band, which sounded pretty good, but that comment snapped her gaze straight to his. "We have some decent restaurants in California." She paused. "But there aren't many close to where I call home."

He'd caught the surprise that widened her eyes but gave her credit for a quick response in spite of that. He also noted she'd avoided addressing the more personal aspect of his comment.

"California girl, huh?" He felt the pinch of disappointment. California was a hell of a long way. "Close to your mother, I guess."

"Nope, Northern California. Hill country. That's as close to the movie sets as I care to live."

"Is that where most of your work is? Movie sets?"

"Most, yes, but on location, not in studio, so pretty much all over the place. I've also worked a few of the big rodeos with some already scheduled this fall, spotlight entertainer and that sort of thing. This is my first historical reenactment. I've got an offer for a WWII reenactment mid-summer but haven't accepted it yet. It's an interesting concept, these reenactments, but I have to see how well all of this will suit me and my horses."

"How did you end up in stunt work rather than acting?"

"Love of horses. Love of riding." She shrugged. "And took after my dad, I guess." She hesitated. "Kent West."

Wolf whistled softly. The man was as famous in his own right as Madeline Breck was in hers, with seven straight world records riding broncs as a rodeo professional before turning Hollywood stuntman. As far as the tabloids had it, Kent West had been *almost killed* in everything from doubling in a street car race scene to diving from a cliff as a pirate. "Just how *much* do you take after him?"

"Well, I'm not suicidal." Her tone held a note of ruefulness. And something else as well.

"Glad to know my services won't be needed." Keep it light was all he knew to do if he didn't want to push his way into that *something else*. And he didn't. At least not here and now. And not this way.

She tilted her head to one side at the comment. "Your services? As a U.S. Marshal?"

"I'm also a licensed psychologist."

She leaned back in her chair as the waitress arrived with their food. But, once they were served, she picked right back up on his words and he didn't think her interest was feigned. "Psychologist. How did *that* happen?"

"My parents chose to live off the Boundary but most of our family, on both sides, live on the land trust. One of my cousins got into drugs in his early teens. He was the youngest of six boys, a late-in-life afterthought, always hungry for attention in a crowded household. My uncle Ed dragged him into treatment more than once, but he ended up leaving a note and shooting up one last massive dose on his twenty-first birthday. He was supposed to have been with me that night. My uncle is still pissed at me that he wasn't."

"It's easier for him to be angry at you than at his son. Not rational but easier."

He shrugged. "I've learned grief isn't rational. His death, what it did to his family, made enough of an impression on me that I thought psychology, helping young people, was what I wanted to do."

"You found out different?"

He nodded. "Pretty much by accident. Got called in on a county trial as an expert witness. After that, I was hooked on getting the bad guys who were tearing down kids. But I didn't want to be part of any *good old boys'* sheriff's department." For sure not one run by his ex-brother-in-law. "I looked around and saw professionalism I could admire in the Marshals Service so that's where I headed. I still use my college training to work with young people but not on a clinical basis. I help with an afterschool sports program that includes pretty much everything but football."

"On the land trust?"

"On and off. Cherokee and non. Teenagers are teenagers and most of their internal struggles aren't related to their DNA." He hesitated. "On the side, I ride herd on a half dozen or so teenaged boys." He'd exposed more of himself than he intended, but it didn't feel as risky as it once would have. Not with Kylah.

When the waitress returned to clear their plates, she asked if they'd like another drink. Wolf glanced toward Kylah then nodded.

When she walked away, Kylah looked at him and took

a deep breath. "Five years ago, my husband committed suicide."

Wolf didn't know what he'd expected her to say, but it wasn't that. He felt gut-punched at the thought of what she'd endured. And at the thought that his competition was a dead man. No winning that one. "I'm sorry," he said and meant it.

"Looking back, I think he was manic-depressive or something similar. At twenty-seven, all I knew was I was marrying the love of my life. Marty was a stuntman, like my dad. Always a clown, always looking for that next high. Two years later he was dead."

Holy cow. He'd read about Marty Davis. The man had died acting as a double in what proved to be one of the top-grossing movies of the decade. Wolf had made a rare trip to the movie theater to watch the high-profile action film about a military rescue of several abducted children, young sons and daughters of political figures held for ransom. During a scene that was supposed to involve a last-minute parachute opening inside a jungle compound, the guy never pulled the ripcord. There were people on the ground close enough to see that he made no effort and slammed into the ground with eyes open and a peaceful expression. The scene had never been re-taken and, in the end, the movie was completed without it.

"At first, I didn't believe them when they called it suicide. Then I found the note he left for me. It was tucked into my daily planner a couple of weeks ahead." She took a deep breath that ended on a small shudder. "For a long time, I was devastated. Then, I was mad as hell at him."

"And now?"

"Two days ago was the anniversary of his death, and

I realized I couldn't remember him, not the way I thought I always would. And, I guess, a part of me decided five years was long enough for … whatever. I went 'looking for love in all the wrong places' as the song and the saying goes." She gave a humorless laugh. "That didn't get me much beyond a hangover."

Wolf reached across the table and closed his hand around hers. "Let's leave the vote open on that one, shall we?"

* * *

What a sad tale. And what a sad thing these humans do to themselves and to the people who love them. But I begin to think these two just might form a bond. I'm of the opinion that Kylah can take care of herself. She has a strength that wasn't evident in our first unfortunate evening together. Even with that, I've found many humans do better with a partner. Not that Jake is a bad chap but Kylah might like someone more than a hired hand who is also a pal. None of which is as important as figuring out who murdered Maisy McGuire.

Our waitress approaches, carrying what is doubtless the bill for our meal in a little folder. Time for me to decide where I want to sleep tonight. Kylah's room is very comfortable but makes it hard for me to come and go as I prefer. Yet, I think, for tonight she may appreciate my presence. Besides, I want to hang with her to be sure I get a closeup view of tomorrow's dress rehearsal of this epic reenactment. There will be people out and about and maybe even a clue I can uncover regarding our ongoing investigation.

A pair of nice, leather hiking boots stops inches from our table and breaks my line of thought. I shift positions for a better view.

* * *

"You were at the meeting this afternoon, at the college."

Wolf glanced up from paying the check and frowned slightly. Kylah found herself pinned in the stare of a young man who stood close to their table, too close. His shoulder was to Wolf, his focus on Kylah. His long, thin nose would be handsome one day. For now, it was more than his other features could handle with any kind of symmetry. "You were holding a cat and sitting with the outsiders. The cat made me notice you."

"He's certainly striking," she said evenly.

"You're one of the reenactors."

"And you came in with the student council." She studied him a moment. "And, yes, Mr. McDaniel, I will take part in the event."

Wolf shifted in his chair, and Kylah glanced across at him. His hardened expression warned he was about take issue with the kid's accusatory tone, and she shook her head slightly. So far, the boy, because that's what he was, hadn't so much as glanced Wolf's way. Kylah suspected he should have.

"I guess you're like the rest. You don't care that you've put us all in danger."

"Danger? To you? Are you frightened?" Kylah's tone held mild curiosity. She—no more than Wolf, by his expression—thought the kid was afraid. His dark eyes glittered with emotion, but it wasn't fear.

"Shouldn't I be? People getting killed and all."

"Not people," Kylah corrected him. "A woman. With a name and a life and people who loved her. Your attempt to turn a tragedy into a stage drama is distasteful and gets you no sympathy from me. You're wasting your time."

"Well, all of you might want to be real careful at that dress rehearsal. Seems somebody besides a bunch of college kids is upset about you reenactors coming here."

Wolf, it seemed, had had enough. He stood, the action pulling the young man's gaze to him. "Since you're scared, how about I call your dad and have him come take you home where you'll feel safer?"

The younger man's eyes widened. "Waya. I didn't see you. No, man, I'm good." He nodded at Kylah and turned on his heels. His exit was far more hurried than his entrance.

Kylah looked up at Wolf. "Waya? Cherokee?"

He held out his hand and waited until she stood and placed hers in it. "Cherokee."

"For Wolf. Of course," she murmured. "And who *was* that?"

"That would be a cousin once removed, one of Ed's grandkids."

"Is he pissed at you, too?"

"Dusty? Not that I know. I'm surprised he even recognized me. Like most kin, we see each other at funerals and weddings. As far as I can tell, there isn't much of anything or anyone that he likes. He just needs to grow up. He's been battling his way out of his own wet blanket for years."

"He seems harmless enough."

Wolf held the door open for her as they walked out. "But irritating as hell. What is it about this dress rehearsal that's got him riled up?"

Kylah left her hand in Wolf's as they walked toward the truck. She could feel the calluses on his palm. She took a deep breath. "As best I can tell, it's an opportunity for the organizers to make sure all of the costumes and props are authentic before the paying audience arrives. Maybe Dusty doesn't think the Cherokee will be fairly or accurately represented. Or maybe he's just a kid in need of a target for his growing pains."

He cocked one brow, and she realized again how sexy the man was. "The dress rehearsal … that's coming up soon, I take it?"

"Tomorrow. Our first live scenes are scheduled for Saturday. We need to know we're ready."

"What about your costume? Authentic enough to make Grant happy?"

Kylah lifted a brow. "Are you kidding? I have access to some of the best historical wardrobes in the world."

"Ah, yes, the movie studios."

They stopped by the passenger door to Wolf's truck, but he didn't open it right away. Her heart thudded in the silence, so loud she was sure he could hear it, and then he said, "You know, I hadn't thought about it before, but it may be odd that Maisy McGuire was dressed out in her costume when she was killed. It was kind of early for that, wasn't it?"

Kylah bit her lip. What an idiot she was. Her thoughts had been on his lips while his had been on a dead woman.

"Maybe. Something to consider for sure," she murmured.

Wolf must have heard something odd in her voice because he tilted his head. "What is it?"

Kylah let herself laugh, and it felt good. "When you stopped and didn't say anything, I thought you were going to kiss me. I was thinking about how that would feel, and you were thinking about murder."

Wolf stepped closer, and she found herself pinned between him and the truck. "I like your train of thought much better." He tilted her chin with one hand and brushed her lips with his. "And I'm happy to show you how that kiss feels." And then he did.

He didn't rush, and her arms twined around his neck. She could feel the length of his body against hers, could feel his reaction to her, to the kiss. With a reluctance that bemused her, she pulled back enough to tell him, "I'm not sure I'm ready for much more than this."

He leaned his forehead to hers. "Do you want to be?"

"Yes," she admitted.

"I'll take that. For now." And he kissed her again.

Chapter 9

*M*y, oh, my! This place does seem to be in chaos this morning. Jake and Kylah sit outside the horse trailer with their mugs of coffee, staring glumly at the comings and goings. The arena is filled with what Kylah called day trippers, people who bring horses unused to crowds and the sound of gunfire. Those skittish animals create a hazard for anyone around them. Kylah has no intention of bringing her animals out of their stalls until the crowds are gone, which means she'll be in the arena late tonight giving them their daily exercise.

I sense her tension over the day ahead. It's because of that and my watchfulness that I see her straighten as a figure in costume passes by. I get up when she does, prepared to follow, if only to alleviate the boredom of watching humans who haven't a clue what they're supposed to be doing as they try to find someone who can enlighten them.

* * *

"Ella? Ella Necaise?"

The person hesitated and turned, and Kylah saw she was right. It was Maisy McGuire's partner. Kylah wasn't sure what she was going to say, but it didn't seem right to ignore the grieving woman.

Ella, dressed as Kylah was in era-appropriate men's attire, stopped and waited for Kylah to reach her. Her expression was controlled, but her eyes were bleak and Kylah's heart hurt for her.

She touched the sleeve of Ella's uniform. "I wanted you to know that I'm sorry for your loss."

"I appreciate that." Her glance moved to Kylah's cheek. "You still have a bruise."

"It doesn't hurt." And it didn't. And no need for Ella to know her panicked arrival had sent that rock flying into her face. "Is there ... is there anything I can do for you? To help you?"

Ella looked lost, and her words said as much. "I don't know what to do." She hesitated. "But, yeah, maybe. The investigators won't let me have—they haven't released Maisy's body to me." Tears brightened her eyes, but she blinked to keep them from falling. "But our campsite—the barricade can come down now. They're finished. I'm going there now. You could go with me?"

"Of course." What a hard, hard thing to have to do alone, Kylah thought. "What about family or friends? Is anyone coming to help with arrangements?"

"We don't have family. At least none that will speak to us." She stopped and took a deep breath. Kylah suspected she was realizing all over again there was no more *us*.

"I've talked with a funeral service here. Maisy wanted to be cremated. We both wanted that for ourselves. I never imagined I'd have to deal with it so soon."

Ella turned away and started walking, and Kylah glanced back at Jake to be sure he saw she was leaving the area and going with Ella. He gave her a nod, his gaze tracking to the cat at her heels.

She caught up to Ella with a few long strides, and they walked together in silence. The women's campsite looked forlorn in the morning mist. The investigators could at least have returned to remove the barricade which lay as much on the ground as not. Ella compressed her lips at the scene and began rolling up the yellow tape in stoic silence.

Kylah took it from her. "I'll do that. You'll want to check your belongings."

The other woman yielded the roll she'd started, her eyes not meeting Kylah's. Kylah watched her duck into the tent and sighed. In a few moments, she had the tape rolled with a loop-back tie to keep it secure. Not a sound came from within the tent. Uncertain what to do next, she watched as the cat walked a blurred line of what looked like spray paint on the ground behind a small, crudely built table. Realization hit her with a chill as Callahan stirred a section of the line with a front paw.

Kylah broke a branch from a low-growing bush and joined him in brushing back and forth across the faint remainder of the outline of the young woman's body who had died here so violently. Her partner had likely seen it already, but, even if she had, there was no reason for the woman to have to deal with it. Sheriff Mitchell, or someone, was going to hear from Kylah about this.

There was little to do after that except wait for Ella to

emerge. Callahan sniffed at the cold remains of a campfire and a kettle that appeared to hold some type of beans, cold and congealed.

She hadn't long to wait. Ella was composed as she stepped out of the tent. Her glance took in the campsite, touched upon the ground where Kylah and Callahan had done their best to obliterate the paint outline of her dead partner. But paint was paint, and traces remained.

"Thank you," Ella said. Grief had etched its lines onto her face.

"I noticed, of course, that you're in uniform. Do you plan to go on with the reenactment?"

Ella's chin lifted. "Yes. I'm doing it for Maisy." She hesitated, "And I don't know what else to do. There's nothing for me to go home to. It would be difficult to go back to work for now. I can't concentrate. I thought I'd keep my vacation for the next week as planned, stay here until I can take Maisy's ashes home."

A too-familiar bleakness swept through Kylah. "Would you like to move from here? We'll help you."

Ella looked around. "No. Maisy liked this spot. I'll stay."

"Tell me about her." Kylah knew the need to talk about loss. "Tell me about Maisy."

For the first time, Ella's expression lightened. The change was faint but it was there. She righted a toppled stool and brought Kylah another from inside the tent. They sat together, and Ella talked--how they'd met, how they'd fallen in love. Kylah listened without judgement. She understood love. And she understood loss.

"Maisy had never been in a reenactment. I'd become a little bit of a pro at it, at least the Indian-Settler ones, all a lot better organized than what I've seen here. But I know this is the town's first, so …" She took a long breath, no doubt overwhelmed by the memories flooding her mind. "One was in her hometown, and she came to watch. We ended up in the same bar after the last performance on the final day. I was still in uniform and a hot mess because it was the middle of summer, which sucks when you're dressed in wool for these things, but its prime time for pulling an audience. Maisy's a Civil War buff, and she walked right up to me and started talking. Seems like we never quit talking." Her smile held a deep sadness. "I'll miss her forever."

Kylah thought about the way she mixed past and present tense when talking about her partner. It would be a while before the reality sank in and, yes, Ella would miss her forever. Kylah prayed she would also find the strength to move on and make a good life for herself. "Was this your first reenactment, together?"

"No, we did a couple last year, but Maisy wanted to get in on a Civil War one. This one popped up when she was online one day. She was so excited and smooth-talked me into it. Not that it took much persuasion. I was game to try something different."

Ella seemed to run out of words. "People didn't understand us. And they didn't like us. But I don't see why anyone would have hurt her. I just don't."

"They didn't like your lifestyle?"

"*That* wasn't even it. There are like two facets of reenactors. Maisy and I are purists. Some call us stitch counters." She grimaced. "Those in the mainstream think we go overboard with our attention to authentic detail. Some purists try to push that preference onto others but Maisy and I," she gave a little sigh, "we care about it for ourselves, and what others do is their business."

"That's why she was already in uniform then?"

"Yes, we're always dressed out when we're on camp site. We change to go into town and all, but here," she looked around, "we're in character always. For us, that's part of the fun of it. Maisy did a lot of digging into old records, census reports and stuff like that, and found she'd lost ancestors from both sides of the war. We brought two sets of uniforms so we could alternate wearing Union blue and Confederate gray colors. I'm still going to do that. For her."

"I didn't think you could do that," Kylah questioned. "I was told pick one or the other and turn it in. The only reason I'm dressed as Confederate is because those were the uniforms the studio had that fit me best and didn't need alteration. I could have cared less."

Ella smiled faintly. "We were kinda sneaky about it. We registered with two commanders, one Rebel, one Yankee, and used our first names for one and middle names for the other. We're foot soldiers so, what the hell, they'll never sort us out from the dozens of others."

Kylah could picture it. She sat thinking in silence, and Ella watched her until she suggested, "Maybe it wasn't who Maisy was or how she felt, North or South, purist or mainstream. Maybe it was somebody who's mad about the reenactment, and Maisy was just ... here."

"There are always people who don't like reenactments in their town, but to hurt my Maisy over it? To take her from me?"

"I guess it can feel a little like an invasion of their home, to some. I don't know. And some people are very passionate about war, whether for or against."

"But this is history, and history is important. I don't

know how many times I've heard, and said, if the human race doesn't remember and learn from our mistakes, we're bound to repeat them. War is ugly, but it's a valuable lesson in the failings of humans."

"And in their greed and their hatred."

"That, too," Ella agreed. She got to her feet. "Thank you for talking to me. For listening."

Kylah stood, and Callahan twined around her boots. She held out her hand to Ella. "I'll be here through the end of the event. If you need anything, let me know. Or Jake. We'll help with whatever."

Ella shook her hand and nodded, then took a deep breath and walked back into the empty tent she'd shared with Maisy.

Kylah looked down at Callahan. "This sucks." And they headed back to Jake and her horses.

* * *

What a way with words these humans have. And what a lot I have to ponder. I agree with Ella. Nothing's adding up. There are far too many theories for who murdered Maisy, and why they might have done so, but none of them very strong.

I also agree with the essence of Kylah's comment. There's nothing about this murder that seems fair or deserved. I'm of the opinion that some people need a good killing. And I'm also aware that sounds harsh, but I've seen more than my share of the ugliness that can sometimes be found in human nature. But nothing I've heard suggests that was the case with Maisy McGuire. And, yet, someone felt that she was one of those who needed killing.

* * *

They were halfway back when Kylah decided she was not a fan of Civil War era clothing. At least not the military uniforms. She had no idea what the fabric was but it was hot and scratchy and bunchy in all sorts of uncomfortable places. She supposed it would be warm in the winter but, dear Lord, it would have to be suffocating in the heat of summer. With the weather mid-season, it was bearable but barely.

And the knapsack she had on her back was a real miss. She should have thought to set it aside before coming with Ella. It wasn't large and didn't have much in it, but it was heavy in its own right. She couldn't imagine carrying the weight of it filled with actual provisions for a wartime march.

She heard Callahan yowl in the same instant she felt something spin her off balance. Staggering and disoriented for a moment, she thought the cat had leaped upon her back. But, no, when she regained her balance, he was there at her feet. Still yowling, with his back to Kylah as he faced the woods they'd just left. His yowl dropped to a low moan and another kind of sound reached her, like the sound of a bullet dropping into a revolver chamber. But that was a sound she'd heard only in the movies or on set. The thought repeated itself in her head ... only in the movies. Callahan yowled again, in warning or in anger. She dropped to the ground and accepted the sound she heard was that of a second shot being fired. At her. To her consternation, the cat bounded away into the woods. "Callahan! No!"

* * *

I stop in uncharacteristic hesitation. Uncharacteristic, for me, anyway. I don't hesitate. I act. However, in this instance, so near to the fairgrounds proper, there are too many people close at hand, and their sounds come from too many directions. I can't be sure of my target, and I'm loath to leave Kylah alone without a clear direction in case the shooter should circle back. Most especially, if she's going to continue to call after me which I wish she would not! Her unwarranted concern for me is a clear revelation to the guilty party that their attempt failed. The sooner I get her to a secure place, the better.

Now would be a good time to employ a few of Dax's saltier swear words. This was no accident and was more than a near miss. The bullet struck the bag Kylah is wearing slung from her shoulders. I cringe at the fact that she was nearly killed while in my care, but at least my warning prevented the second bullet from getting as close as the first. She was smart enough to hit the ground.

Now, how to convey to Wolf that the weapon was a revolver of sorts? I'm not at all certain that Kylah is experienced enough with guns to identify the click of a revolver chamber. I missed it with the first shot, but caught it with the second.

I return to find her brushing dead leaves from her hair. "Is he gone? Or she?"

More proof that she's a smart girl, clever enough to understand I'd have the answer to that. I sit on my haunches and gaze into her eyes to reassure her, and she seems to understand that I wouldn't be sitting still if I thought she needed to be on the run. No, at this point, it's her attacker who's been put to flight, but he can't go far enough or fast enough. This case has now turned personal for me.

Like Kylah, I know the villain could be either male or female, but I can't be bogged down in the semantics of saying he or she at every point. Until proven wrong, I will continue with he.

Our first order of business is to find the spent bullet. The knapsack on her back will have slowed it to some extent and, if—as I suspect—the weapon is another of the many antiques around us, the bullet won't have traveled as far as a modern-day make.

I stand, holding her gaze with mine, and begin scratching around in the dead leaves. Her understanding is faster than I'd hoped as she gets to her feet and begins a scrutiny of the area around her. "Good idea, Callahan. We need to find that bullet."

Kylah pauses in her search and pulls her phone from her pocket to place a call. As she gives our general location and asks for help finding something, I'm amazed at her calm. I wonder if it's Jake or Wolf she's called. My question isn't answered when both arrive, not until I see the questioning look she shoots Jake and the shrug he gives in return.

She addresses them as one as she explains what happened. Their reactions give me a few useful curses to add to my collection. Too bad I can't share them with Dax. I'm happy to hear her describe the sound of the gun as a revolver. Kylah West is more than a pretty face and accomplished equestrian. She knows her guns ... but does she know how to aim and shoot one?

* * *

Wolf couldn't have begun to peg his emotions with any accuracy as he took the knapsack from Kylah's back and examined where the bullet had entered and where it exited. He needed to focus, he warned himself, push the personal aside and think like a lawman. But he wasn't sure how successful he could be, not when he could picture that projectile tearing through the smooth skin and the arteries and organs of the woman standing in front of him. His mind struggled with possibilities. Was this random? Was she a target?

He realized Kylah was staring at him with a startled look in her eyes and knew he'd given himself away. This woman was way more than someone he wanted to kiss again, more than someone he longed to take to bed. Way more, way fast. Maybe even too fast.

"Which direction were you walking?"

She turned toward the fairgrounds, and Wolf turned with her. He could see the roof of the equestrian center, glimpsed the silver metal of the walls through the thin line of trees ahead. "Straight ahead, this way."

"The bullet caught your knapsack at an angle." His voice roughened in spite of his best effort. "You're lucky you were wearing it." He was lucky. "If it hadn't spun you off balance, the second might have been a direct hit."

Kylah turned back to him and nodded. Her eyes were shadowed. "Believe me, that thought has already crossed my mind. But," and he could tell she hesitated before adding, "Callahan's warning helped with that."

She watched as he retrieved his cell phone from his pocket. Les Mitchell was in his favorites list for quick contact, although sure as hell not because he was a personal favorite. Wolf started talking as soon as Les answered. "I have shots fired, no injuries." Thank God. "I'm going to need some officers on the scene to help locate a needle in a haystack. Put a canine with them." He gave their location with the arena as point of reference. "We'll watch for you."

As he disconnected, Jake called out to them. He and Callahan emerged from a low-growing thicket. He held out his hand with a small object in the palm. "I think this may be something we're looking for. Not sure we'll ever find the actual bullet that was shot at her."

Kylah stared at the object in his hand and shook her

head. "I have no idea what that is."

Wolf did. "It's an unused linen cartridge. Either linen or a paper was used to load revolvers before metal cartridges came into use. Metal ones were available during the War Between the States but in short supply and not much used by the common soldier." He'd done some homework after the first shooting.

"You think someone shot at me with a Civil War weapon? Like they did Maisy?" She looked disbelieving.

"Just like," Wolf said, feeling grim, "except this time they missed." And he was hellbent on finding them before there was a next time.

Kylah turned and walked a short distance away, staring into the trees. Wolf knew she was processing things in her mind. He understood the need. He looked down at Callahan. "I don't guess you have a clue you can show me now? Something that will help me keep her safe."

Chapter 10

I'll be darned if I don't feel like a failure. That's not a good feeling for me. A clue is what I don't have.

We withdraw to Kylah's trailer as the sheriff and his men arrive to begin combing the area for any additional evidence. Before they disperse, Wolf takes a moment to show Sheriff Mitchell the intact cartridge. Like me and Jake, Wolf doesn't believe finding the linen cartridge is a coincidence. However, I'm not sure whether it was dropped accidently or intentionally. I applaud Wolf's suggestion that the sheriff caution his men not to broadcast the incident, and more so the fact that the weapon used today was almost certainly another antique. I've seen more than one investigation stalled by a copycat prankster who has his or her own motive for muddying the waters. I hope the deputies find something that will help, another cartridge perhaps, either of the spent bullets, footprints, anything. Not, mind you, that I think they can do better than I can. However, my place is with Kylah at the moment, and my money is on Wolf for helping me solve this case. The sheriff was wisdom itself in bringing him in on an official basis.

Several hours later, they all troop back, and I do my best not to feel smug that they found no more than we did, which is another linen cartridge. It could be a mate to the first or not. Either way it's of no more help at this point than the other.

The sheriff sends his men to begin questioning those in the area as to what they may have seen or heard, and the rest of us remain in Kylah's trailer. With a slide-out opened that I hadn't realized existed, there is more than enough room for us. I note the fact that Wolf pulls Kylah to sit beside him on a small love seat—interesting name, that—and she doesn't balk at his action.

* * *

Les gave Wolf a look that he had no difficulty deciphering. "We need to talk through some things."

Wolf shrugged. "That's fine but since Kylah was the intended victim, and Jake was with me, we can talk it through right here. I don't suppose you've got anything to reveal other than your thoughts and some possibilities, and I've got the same."

Les shook his head. The sheriff didn't look happy, but he yielded the point and started talking. "I'd hoped Maisy McGuire was a murder of passion--barring that, a random killing, even though I knew that was a long shot. With Ella Necaise cleared and someone shooting at Ms. West today, I'm seeing at least two patterns, possibly a third."

He shifted his look from Wolf to Kylah. "Both of you female. Both of you dressed in costumes. And both dressed as men."

Once the sheriff started talking, Jake got up and began making coffee with quiet movements.

Wolf saw Kylah give him a quick smile of thanks before she answered the sheriff. "That's because females weren't allowed into the military at the time."

"Can't think with typical logic here. Anybody that'd shoot a woman in what appears to be cold blood may have their own brand of logic, but you won't be able to match it with sane thinking."

Wolf knew what he was saying. Crazy had logic but it was a logic only crazy understood. In cases like this, looking for patterns was the likeliest method of identifying a killer.

"Both of you would be considered strong-willed," Les pushed forward.

"And you think someone would kill because of that? Because we're strong women?" Kylah looked insulted, and Wolf couldn't blame her.

"Limitless reasons people kill. None of them good." Les rubbed his jaw, thinking. "I'm told Ms. McGuire was called a stitch-counter by some, and it wasn't a compliment."

"No, it isn't," Kylah agreed. "A stitch-counter or purist is someone considered over-the-top about the need to stay in character. And as far as your patterns go, yes, my uniform is one hundred percent authentic, and I have stayed in character all morning, even to keeping my cap on and hair hidden. But if someone's been watching me, they'd know this is the first time I've been in costume since I got here. From what Ella told me, she and Maisy were always in costume from the moment they stepped foot on the site."

Jake put a saucer of milk in front of Callahan, then

began handing out mugs of coffee, placing sugar, creamer, and spoons on the table, but he'd fixed Kylah's for her with cream and sugar. Wolf had paid attention to how much because he planned to make use of the knowledge some morning. Given the chance.

The sheriff took an appreciative sip from his cup before answering Kylah's last comment. "I'll admit this person may have been just walking around today looking for the next target."

"That seems improbable," Wolf injected. "Doesn't it?"

Les agreed. "Improbable but still possible."

Wolf was watching Les' eyes. There was something the sheriff didn't want to say, and Wolf had a pretty good idea what it was. "What's your third possible pattern?"

Les glanced his way. "Maisy McGuire and Ella Necaise shared a lifestyle which sets some people off. And, from what Ms. West has said, she was coming back from Ms. Necaise's campsite, and she'd been there for some time. The two of them alone together."

"Which I wouldn't have needed to be if your team hadn't left a grieving woman to clean up a damned crime scene," Kylah returned. "What were you thinking?"

Les closed his eyes for a brief moment, looking chagrined at her words. "I hadn't realized. I'm sorry for that. It will be addressed, and Ms. Necaise will receive an apology."

Apparently mollified by his sincerity, Kylah's expression turned thoughtful. "We were out in the open in front of the tent in plain view the whole time. But it could be the shooter either watched us walking to her camp and me coming back alone sometime later. Or, he chanced on us alone in front of her camp and then followed me."

"Either way," Les agreed, looking relieved that she wasn't going to get in a twist over his premise. They couldn't rule out any possibility at the moment.

Wolf knew it could never be easy to tell a person they could be a potential victim on multiple fronts.

"You might as well go on and say the other theory you're looking at," Wolf said in resignation.

"Well, both dressed as men, both with caps on so their hair was hidden. The shooter may not have realized either *was* a woman."

"So, the uniforms could be the reason? Someone antiwar to that extreme?"

"Could be," Les said. "Or could be someone who doesn't like the event itself."

"Like someone from the Boundary." Wolf met the sheriff's glance with a steady eye.

"I have to consider it," Les agreed.

Wolf held his temper. "I agree," he admitted, "and I know there were problems in the past, some not wanting to accept changes that seemed forced on them, but that's been decades ago and those were kids who are grown up now. And the worst of it was graffiti and small vandalism, not murder. The Cherokee aren't living in that past."

The sheriff took another swallow of his coffee. "Insanity lives in whatever world it chooses."

And that was a point Wolf couldn't argue. "So, what now?"

"Now, I'm hoping you can convince Rita to cancel or postpone this event."

Wolf couldn't help the disbelieving snort of laughter that escaped him. "You're not serious."

"Damn it, Wolf! I've got a nut job trying to take people

out with antique weapons. He's been successful once and damn near was again today. No agency could provide enough security at something this big. No way in hell! He could be any one of hundreds of reenactors who are strangers to the area, strangers to the area law enforcement. What do you expect me to do?"

"Try applying a little logic. First off, no one's going to convince Rita to postpone this event, much less cancel it. Second, if someone could, it wouldn't be me. Rita's never listened to me about a thing."

"Then why the hell did you marry her?" Les glared at him.

Wolf lifted his coffee mug in a sarcastic toast. "Might have been the shotgun you had pointed at my back."

"Well, air the dirty laundry, for Christ sakes!"

Wolf grinned. Damned if he could help it. "Old news the entire county knew and forgot years ago." He drained his coffee cup and got to his feet.

His escape wasn't quick enough, and the sheriff got the last poke in when he asked, "What were you doing here today anyway?"

"Just stopped by to check things out, and damned good thing I did."

"Back to my point," Les retorted. "I can post a deputy or two, but they sure as hell can't safeguard hundreds of actors and thousands of visitors over the next two weeks. I need you to talk to Rita."

"I'll go today, but you know as well as I do, she won't budge." He saw the defeated look on Les' face. Damn. "But I'll try."

Wolf put his hand on the doorknob and looked at Kylah. "I'll be back in a bit. You okay?"

She smiled at him, and he wished like hell they were alone for one moment.

"I'm fine. Jake and I are going back to work."

He noticed she didn't respond to his first comment. He supposed he could take it as a positive sign that she didn't say there was no need for him to be back … in a bit or otherwise.

Les followed him out, and Callahan scooted out between them. "Damn it, Wolf, there are times you're a thorn in my side."

"I can remember when that was all of the time and not just some of the time."

His ex-brother-in-law snorted a little at that. "Not that long ago, either." He put his hat on his head. "I'm headed to talk with the man who could be the last person to see Maisy McGuire alive before her murder. And, if he doesn't have a damned good accounting for his whereabouts this morning, he might even be our guy." Les hesitated then added, "You're welcome to come along. I guess Rita can wait a while longer."

Wolf looked down at Callahan then nodded at Les. "Obliged. Hope you don't mind if the cat comes, too."

The sheriff sighed and shook his head. Wolf and Callahan followed him to his patrol car.

* * *

Kylah had wondered why Wolf was at the fairgrounds as well but she wasn't sure she would've asked. Nor was she sure Wolf would have provided a better answer than the casual, "Just stopped by to check things out," he'd offered the sheriff.

She met Jake's steady gaze. "Ready to work?"

For a moment he didn't say anything. "Always ready to work, but … are you sure you want to stay? That was a close call. Could be we should pack up and head home."

"I won't do that. My job is here. But I won't hold it against you if you want to go home."

Jake looked affronted, but the words had to be said. He didn't even bother to respond to her offer. "You going to ride in that get-up?"

She smiled, hoping to ease the insult he felt he'd been dealt. "They've got to get used to it sometime, sooner better than later. I don't want to get dumped on the battlefield."

Not that she thought any of them would buck with her under any circumstances. They were too well trained. To her relief, Jake followed her lead. The corners of his eyes crinkled in a smile as he finished his coffee. "Might as well get started. If there's gonna be a side show, I don't want to miss it."

* * *

What a prime opportunity! I don't always get to sit in on the questioning of a person of interest, particularly not one who might prove to be the actual murderer. I've been in a sheriff's car before, and this one is pretty much run-of-the-mill. No fancy bells and whistles, nothing but the basics, but I have the back seat to myself, and it's comfortable enough.

"So, tell me about this fellow we're going to see," *Wolf suggests.*

I sit up and move to the edge of the seat, the better to hear the exchange. The more information I have, the faster Wolf and I can solve this case.

"Raymond Latimer is with a unit from somewhere up north. Pennsylvania, I think. I've got a file on him in my office. Nothing stood out. He's never been in any trouble. Steady job in some kind of manufacturing plant. Married with two grown children, both in college. Wife's into herb gardening, sells what she grows at a local market every weekend, and seldom leaves home otherwise. His hobby is this type of event, reenacting Civil War battles. He also visits and photographs Civil War cemeteries. Gone most weekends with some historical group or other."

"Huh."

Wolf's grunt mirrors my thoughts. Do these people not have a real life?

"Yeah, well, the frequent separation may be what keeps them married."

A commentary on the sheriff's own marriage? Something to poke at if I had time for such miniscule mysteries as that. Fortunately, I don't. Murder is far more entertaining.

"So, how does this Latimer come into the picture with the deceased?" *Wolf asks.*

"Seems he was the go-between for the sale of the murder weapon," *the sheriff explains.* "We're going to talk with the previous owner and then with Latimer."

"Previous owner a friend of his?"

"Of sorts. He's Latimer's unit commander."

"So, a person with authority and latitude in these surroundings." *I can almost hear the thoughts spinning in Wolf's head.* "Have you considered a gun ring of some sort? Or smuggling of antiques?"

I wish I could see more than the backs of their heads and a bit of profile now and again. Expressions can be very telling.

"Considered it and did a little digging. Nothing pops.

The guy's been a collector for years, goes to big gun shows but buys with caution, sometimes sells. No ties to anyone or anything out of the way so far."

Wolf rubs his neck. "Nothing fits, does it?" *It's a repetition of what's been said before because it's annoyingly true.*

"Nothing at all." *The sheriff agrees, sounding no happier about the fact than Wolf.*

"They both coming to the station?"

"Nope. I have Latimer headed there now. Going to let him cool his heels and sweat, hopefully get a little antsy so that he loses the thread of any story he might have made up."

"You think he's the one?" *Wolf sounds as dubious as I feel.*

"I don't, but I'm too smart to treat him otherwise, until I know otherwise." *I'm not going to admit to being impressed with the sheriff. Not yet.*

"So where are *we* headed now?"

"We're going to drop in unannounced on Commander Fagan, Vance Fagan. My deputies tell me he's inspecting uniforms all day today, so he'll be close to his field quarters."

"Field quarters? I take it you mean his tent. These people take this stuff to heart, don't they?"

"They damn sure do." *I don't think the sheriff's tone is expressing any admiration of the fact.*

The sheriff parks, and we exit the car, and I stretch my legs. The drive was longer than I expected it to be, longer than if we'd trekked across the hills and through the creek, but I somehow don't think the sheriff is inclined to walk anyplace he can drive.

Now that the hordes have moved in, the vista is rather amazing. Reenactors are milling about outside of their tents, garbed in their historic apparel, carrying a wide array of weaponry, everything from handguns to rifles—with and without bayonets—to swords.

Somehow, I hadn't equated sabers with the war between the states, but they doubtless were there or they wouldn't be here. These enthusiasts are authentic to the core. More than the Confederate flags and unit standards flapping in the breeze, more even than the period costumes, it's the military bearing of the reenactors themselves that tell the tale. They're not only in costume, they're in character.

True to the sheriff's expectations, Commander Fagan is close at hand and easy to find. He leads the way to his headquarters through an astonishing number of men in their realistic military attire of another century. He gestures towards a tent that sits on a rise so that it's slightly elevated from the many smaller ones that surround it. Intentional? That's my suspicion.

Inside, it's a true commander's space with a long, crudely built table and an equally rough bench on either side. I catch sight of a wireless printer tucked into the bottom of a bookshelf and surmise a laptop might be secreted in one of the knapsacks scattered about. The glimpse of technology serves as a reminder that this historical reenactment is a jaunt for some but a business to others.

Not, however, a padded chair in sight. Ugh. I settle discreetly on the top shelf, careful to send nothing tumbling to the rug which covers the earth floor beneath us.

"Gentlemen." I note that he extends his hand first to the sheriff who is wearing a badge, then rather offhandedly to Wolf, who is not. Were he more observant, he'd note from Wolf's demeanor that he's twice the leader as the sheriff, who's more of the good old boy mentality. But, he's sharp, I'll give him that. Sheriff Les Mitchell is nobody's fool. "I gather you have questions about the rifle I sold Ms. McGuire before her death."

"You mean before she was murdered."

Now that was crudely done. But I suspect it was as intentional as it was crude.

The commander stiffens and glares at the sheriff. "As you say.

Please sit, gentlemen."

He takes one bench and Wolf and the sheriff take the other, facing him. The commander glances at me on my perch atop the bookshelf, but he says not a word nor does his expression change. Good for him.

Sheriff Mitchell wastes no time getting started on his questions. "Did you know Maisy McGuire?"

"Never met her." *Well, he's not a chatty one, that's for sure.*

"Then how did the sale of your weapon to her come about?"

Wolf appears interested in the exchange, relaxed but interested. On the other hand, the sheriff looks bored with his own questions, though I feel certain that isn't the case.

"Via our communication board. There's always something posted for sale, as well as notices of meetings or outings in whatever town. It's a common practice."

"Outings?" *The sheriff manages to make the word* outings *sound nefarious.*

"Gathering at a pub, a wine tasting, a ghost tour. Anything of interest in or around the town of our current venue."

"What about here. Anything of interest?" *I wince because I'm certain the sheriff has set himself, or at least his town, up for an insult.*

"No, nothing at all."

As I said. Wolf and I exchange glances.

The sheriff scowls and says, "So you posted a for-sale notice about the rifle, and she called you."

"Ms. McGuire sent me a text, and we made the arrangements for the sale in similar fashion."

"How did you pick Raymond Latimer to take it to her?"

"He happened to be walking by when I was texting

with Ms. McGuire. She wanted to see the item, with the intent to buy if she liked what she saw."

Sheriff Mitchell looks more than a little dubious at his words. "You picked him at random? To take a collector's item to a woman you've never met?"

"Hardly random. I've known Raymond for years and knew he could be trusted carrying a valuable rifle to her and bringing a significant amount of cash back to me."

"Why not arrange to meet with her yourself?" *The sheriff is still wearing that frown of faint suspicion.*

The commander hesitates, then blows out an irritated breath of air. "We couldn't make our schedules work for me to take it to her. She insisted I tramp out to that isolated spot she'd chosen to pitch her tent. To be honest, I got the feeling she was being intentionally difficult, maybe to drive the price down. Told me she had her eye on another as well. I didn't want to lose the sale. I knew if she laid eyes on my Burnside, she wouldn't want to lose it."

"Do you have a copy of what you posted?"

The commander leaves the table to rummage through some papers on a surface that appears to suffice as his makeshift desk. He returns with a sheet of paper he hands to the sheriff who reads it and frowns.

"You were selling two rifles?"

"My intention was only to sell one or the other. The Enfield or the Burnside. Buyer's choice."

"That's a pretty good sum for either." *Mitchell hands the paper off to Wolf, who has yet to comment on anything, which I find interesting.* "And I noticed you asked for cash, no checks or credit cards."

"I've been burned a time or two," *the commander admits.* "I set a fair price. Each weapon worth every penny of it, even more in a different market."

The sheriff watches as Wolf studies the flyer. I could see the thoughts clicking through the sheriff's mind in a rather pedestrian fashion before he returned to his questioning. "So … she looked, she liked, and she sent the cash back with Latimer."

"Yes." *Fagan nods in accompaniment of his terse response.*

"You still have it?"

"The money? I can't say for sure. I already had cash here and I've purchased a bayoneted rifle since then. Whether or not I used money from the sale of the Burnside or what I brought with me," *he shrugs,* "I've no way to know for sure."

"Seems quite a risk you take, keeping that much money lying around."

"Could be, but I've never had any difficulty, never been robbed."

"Was the gun loaded when you handed it off to Latimer?"

"With blanks, if anything. I don't own live ammunition for any of the guns I bring to these events."

"You don't hunt?"

"Never been interested in it."

To my surprise, Les looks straight at Wolf and asks, "You got any questions?"

And, at that, Wolf swings his gaze to the commander. "Did you or Raymond Latimer have any reason to kill that woman?"

As we return to the sheriff's car, I acknowledged the tactic had sound merit. A quick delivery of an unexpected question from an unexpected front can sometimes bring unexpected results. I'll bet some of Dirty Harry's more complex cases were solved in just such a manner when an unprepared response delivers a clue. But not this time. The commander's simple no carried the ring of truth. And I'm sure he realized we'd now be asking similar questions of Raymond Latimer. The more interesting thing to me was that the sheriff and Wolf choreographed it without words. Very skillful. I appreciate the opportunity to watch professionals in action.

Then again, this direct line of questioning may have lost them the ability to keep secret the fact that the carbine Commander Fagan sold Ms. McGuire was the gun that was used to murder her. The question wasn't asked or answered, but it's inevitable that Fagan will come to the only logical conclusion.

* * *

The sheriff stared through the windshield at Fagan's tent. "So? What do you think?"

"Me?" Wolf shook his head. "I don't think there's anything there. No collusion. No motive."

Les grunted and started the car. "Me either. More's the pity. Still doesn't mean Latimer didn't pull that trigger."

"I won't argue the point, but it doesn't ring a bell for me. Maybe he had a grudge against Ms. McGuire, but that doesn't explain the shots fired at Kylah this morning."

"Random?"

"Random. Coincidence. Either's a possibility but not likely. Not for me."

"Me either." Les gave him a sideways glance. "Kylah? Not Ms. West?"

"Mind your own damn business, Les."

His ex-brother-in-law grinned and pulled onto the main road, gunning the motor a bit as they headed back toward town.

Chapter 11

Raymond Latimer surged to his feet when the sheriff opened the door without a warning tap. The man was nervous. There were no two ways about it. Wolf could see it in his eyes as Latimer shifted his focus from the sheriff to Wolf and back again. But being nervous didn't mean he was guilty. Didn't mean he was innocent, either, Wolf reminded himself.

Wolf scanned the room where Latimer had been left for more than an hour, alone with the quiet and his thoughts. Almost filled by the table and four chairs, deliberately uncomfortable, even intimidating in its starkness. He'd been told that the sheriff had been delayed. Not that the delay had been intentional.

Although Les considered it unlikely that Latimer had

murdered the woman, Wolf knew that fact wouldn't affect how the sheriff handled the questioning. "I want him on edge," Les had commented as they walked from the car. Once again, this was the sheriff's interview. He had the lead. All Wolf had to do was listen and observe and be prepared to give his thoughts afterward unless the sheriff signaled him to step in as he'd done earlier.

Latimer was still in his costume as the organizers had required for that day's inspection. Wolf wondered if that was because he hadn't had his turn and received an all-clear on authenticity or because he was enough of an enthusiast that he loved wearing it, given the chance. He suspected either could be the case. The man's build was average—average height, average weight. More muscle than paunch but not too much muscle. An active man, an outdoor man by his weathered face.

Les offered his hand, and Latimer wiped his palm on his sleeve before taking it. Yeah, nerves big-time.

They all took a seat, and Wolf watched as Latimer's stare tracked each of them: the sheriff, Wolf himself, and Callahan. His look lingered longest on the cat, and Wolf could read his confusion, but he held his tongue. Waiting on them. Canniness or trepidation or plain bewilderment? Wolf couldn't tell.

"Where were you this morning?" Les waded right into his questions.

"Huh?" Now it was confusion, plain and simple. He was that easy to read.

"This morning," Les said, sounding patient. "How did you spend the morning?"

"Cleaning my weapons. Me and some buddies. Took them apart, polished them, put them back together. Mine didn't need it but some of theirs did." Latimer shook his head. "People don't take care of their stuff like they should."

"How long did that take?"

Latimer scratched the side of his head. "We didn't rush. We were all waiting for the commander's visual on our uniforms and such. Some hours, right after daylight pretty much until I left to come here."

"Your buddies can account for your whereabouts?" Les' tone was still neutral.

"Sure, but–" Latimer fell silent, closed his mouth, lips pressed together. Wolf thought that odd. If the man had questions, why didn't he ask them?

"I'll need their names before you leave."

"Yes, sir," Latimer said.

Les shot Wolf a look he had no problem interpreting. Les hadn't been looking hard at Latimer, but he'd been looking. So far, he wasn't finding anything, but he wasn't done.

"You look like a person who enjoys the outdoors. Not just for these events?" Les gave his suspect an up-and-down searching look.

Latimer nodded.

"You a hunter?" he asked.

"I hunt, yes, sir."

"I like squirrel hunting myself." Les leaned back in his chair as if relaxing for a nice chat. "You?"

"Some. Mostly deer though. Still hunting. No sport in running dogs."

"Yeah? Ever been out West? Some of the big game stuff?"

"Colorado a time or two. Wyoming once."

"What'd you think of it?"

Latimer hunched his shoulders. "I didn't care for it much. I hunt for food, not sport. Didn't like the feel of it, the attitude of the guides, but I can't explain better than that."

The man still hadn't relaxed. Wolf didn't think Les was going to be able to make that happen. Les seemed to have reached the same conclusion.

"You ever watch a deer bleed out up close? Watch their eyes go dim?"

Latimer paled at the question. Something there, Wolf was sure of it, but what? The sheriff saw it, too—Wolf could tell by the gleam of awareness in his eyes—but he didn't comment on it. He glanced at Wolf before crossing his arms and leaning back in his chair, his gaze fixed on Latimer's features.

But all Latimer did was clear his throat before answering the sheriff. "No, sir." His voice was low and quiet. "Never have."

Wolf cleared his throat, bringing Latimer's attention over to him. "I'm sure you've realized that you may have been the last person to see Maisy McGuire alive."

"Before she was killed, you mean."

"Of course."

"Yes, sir. I've thought about that."

"Why don't you walk us through that morning?"

Latimer had been leaning forward a bit, with hands on the table in front of him, as he and Les had exchanged comments on hunting. He shifted back in his seat at the question, pulled his hands into his lap. Wolf couldn't see if they were clenched together, but he wondered.

"Yes, sir. The commander asked me to take a rifle for Ms. McGuire to look at, said she might want to buy it. He told me how much and said no haggling. She either paid the full amount or I brought the rifle back to him."

"Did you shoot the rifle on the way to deliver it?" Like the sheriff had done, Wolf kept his tone impartial.

"No, sir. Wanted to, though." Did Latimer hesitate before he answered? Wolf wasn't sure. "I don't get to hold many that sweet."

"The commander buys and sells a lot, does he?"

"I wouldn't know about that. His business."

Wolf nodded. "True enough. Keep going."

"Not much else. Ms. McGuire liked the rifle and gave me the money, and I left."

"Did you count the money?"

"Sure. I didn't know her from Adam's housecat. She could as easily have shorted the commander and made me look like a thief."

"You have any reason to believe she would have? Past dealings?" The sheriff shot the question across the table.

"No, sir. Like I said, I didn't know her. Never laid eyes on her until that morning."

"What was she wearing? As much detail as you can. Anything could be important." Wolf made his voice easy, calm.

Latimer looked down, closed his eyes in concentration. "She was dressed out, full uniform. Cap and everything, even early as it was."

"What was the time?" Les interjected.

He looked at the sheriff. "I can't for sure say a time. Was still dark when I started walking across the hills."

"Why that early?" Wolf suspected the whole reenactment scenario wasn't for people who liked to sleep in, but still …

"Commander asked me to go before we started our morning drill. It wasn't no hardship for me. Daylight's my favorite time of day. Watched the sun rise over the hills as I walked."

As Wolf and Les tossed the volley of questions between them, Latimer took his time answering, kept his tone controlled.

"Was she in her tent when you got there?" Wolf asked the question in the same tone he might ask about the weather.

Latimer shook his head and seemed to hesitate. "She was at the cookfire, stirring something in a kettle."

"Breakfast?"

Latimer shrugged. "Couldn't tell."

And not interested, Wolf thought. "What else can you tell us about her camp? What did you notice?"

"Not much. Little table by the cookfire. A bench. No, a stool, I think. Sorry, I wasn't focused on that."

"What were you focused on?" Les asked, his tone unexpectedly sharp. Intentionally so, Wolf suspected.

Latimer shifted his attention back to the sheriff. Tensing. He'd decided who the bad cop was. Had to be the question about watching a deer bleed out, Wolf thought. Les had overdone that one.

"Making the exchange and getting back for morning drill." He stopped, looked apologetic. "If I'd known what was going to happen to her, that it'd be important, I woulda paid more attention to the small stuff."

It was a reasonable answer. "Okay, let's keep on with what you did notice," Wolf said. "She was in full uniform. She had a campfire going. There was a table with a stool. That about it?"

"Yes, sir."

"Did you shake hands with her?"

"Huh?"

"Did you and Ms. McGuire introduce yourselves, shake hands, sit down at that little table?"

"Uh, no. None of that. It was quicker. Most women don't offer their hand to shake, and if they don't, I don't."

"And she didn't, so you didn't. Right?"

"That's right."

"And you didn't sit down?"

"She didn't ask me to. So, no."

"Was she rude, then?"

"I didn't take it that way. I wasn't there for a visit and chit-chat. It was a business deal and not even mine. She was businesslike and so was I."

"Fair enough."

"Did she ask to hold the rifle, examine it? Or did you offer it to her?" Les broke the silence he'd held during that brief exchange.

Latimer turned back toward the sheriff. This time, Wolf could see real hesitation before he answered. "Neither one. She pulled the money from a pocket and held it out to me. I stepped closer."

"Closer to what? Where was she then? The cookfire?"

"No, she—uh—had walked to the little table. She was on one side, and I was on the other." He stopped abruptly.

"Go on."

"Like I said, she pulled the money from her pocket and held it out to me. I put the rifle on the table and counted the money."

"And you still didn't shake hands over the deal."

"Like I said, not my deal."

Les drummed his fingers on the table and looked at Wolf who asked, "Did you think it odd that she'd be carrying that much money in her pocket?"

"No. That's what I'd have done. I'd have it with me, not taken a chance of letting someone see where I kept it when it wasn't on me."

Wolf supposed that made sense.

"And you didn't think it odd that she didn't examine the rifle before paying for it? Didn't even hold it in her hands."

"Not what I would have done," Latimer agreed.

"So, you put the rifle on the table, she handed you the money, and you left. That about it?"

"After I counted it? Yes, sir. That's about it."

"On your way back to camp, after you made the exchange, did you hear shots fired?

"Yes, sir, more than once but as far as I could tell they came from ahead of me, not behind me and not close. I thought it was someone hunting." He looked uncertain then shrugged. "Of course, my hearing's not what it used to be."

"Anything else you can think of we need to know?"

"No, sir."

Latimer looked relieved at what he took as an indication that the end of his grilling was near.

And Wolf supposed it was. Something was off with the whole exchange, but he couldn't say whether it was Latimer's information or Maisy McGuire's behavior during her purchase of a weapon that had ended up being used to kill her. But Les wasn't ready to go public with the fact that the antique was the murder weapon. Wolf wouldn't have either. There were too many unknowns. Too much at stake.

More so with the attempt on Kylah.

But Les wasn't quite through with Latimer even though he signaled an end to the questioning by getting to his feet. Latimer did the same, prepared to follow the sheriff out of the room. But Les stopped at the door and turned back. "I hear you have a peculiar hobby."

Wolf couldn't see Latimer's expression, but he could see the tensing of his spine. "Sir?"

"Hanging around old cemeteries. Strikes me as kinda morbid." Wolf could tell he didn't expect much of a response as he added, "Don't leave town, Latimer," and turned and walked away.

Wolf spoke to a few of the deputies then stopped at the door to Les' office. The sheriff was on his feet, staring out his window, but either sensed or heard Wolf. He turned around.

"I didn't get much out of that."

"No," Wolf agreed.

"But something's there. Something he's not saying."

And Wolf had to agree with that as well. "I'll take Rita your request this afternoon. I don't think you'll get much out of that either."

"No." The sheriff looked morose. "I expect not." He reached for his hat. "Come on. I'll take you back to your truck." He looked down. "You and the cat."

* * *

Without a doubt, something's off-kilter. And, like Wolf and the sheriff, I can't put my paw on it. Something nagged at the back of my mind as I visualized the scene evolving as Raymond Latimer described it. Something I can't quite grasp as yet. I will, of course. I just hope it's in time to help nail the murderer before he, or she, can strike again.

Now, it's decision time again. Do I visit the ex-wife with Wolf or remain to watch Kylah and her clever horses? Choices, choices.

And isn't it interesting that Wolf checks out the arena before heading to see the sheriff's sister?

* * *

Kylah felt his gaze on her. She couldn't have said how she knew it was Wolf, as there had been a sprinkling of people throughout the afternoon, climbing up into the bleachers to watch for a few minutes, some hanging around longer, as she put her horses through a series of maneuvers. But she knew, and when she stepped down from the final workout, she glanced around to prove it to herself.

Wolf met her at the roll-up door of the arena. "Things been quiet here this afternoon?"

She smiled. "Haven't had to dodge a single bullet." As his eyes darkened, she regretted making the comment. He was still far more disturbed about the incident than she was. She had relegated it to the back of her mind, and it had begun to seem more surreal than real to her. "I'm fine."

"I like what you're wearing."

She glanced down. Jeans and long-sleeve tee. Her favorite attire. When she brought her gaze back up to his, one brow lifted, he shrugged.

"The sheriff asked me to run an errand. I thought you might want to ride with me and see a bit of the countryside. It's a pretty drive."

She thought of all the reasons she shouldn't, why it

wasn't a good idea, but when she opened her mouth she said, "That sounds nice. Thank you."

Her wary side reminded her that she'd be in his world no more than another few weeks, cautioned that things were moving in a direction they didn't need to go, advised it was too soon for her, too fast. They'd known each other two days, had dinner together two evenings. To appease that side of her, she waved Jake away, unsaddled the horse, then told Wolf she was ready. Dressed as she was and dusty from riding. But *I like what you're wearing* he'd said.

Jake groomed a different horse in the next stall, and Kylah stopped to let him know she was leaving.

"She'll be with me," Wolf told him and Kylah couldn't tell if it was meant as a challenge or a reassurance. Judging by the look on Jake's face, she suspected he was no more certain than she. Either way, it sounded ... possessive.

She should say something about it, she thought, but she didn't want to make more of it than was warranted. Liar, a little voice whispered from deep inside, and she knew at least a part of her *was* ready and wanted to see where this could go. When had she lost her courage? Had it died with Marty? Had she scattered it with his ashes?

They got into the truck, the three of them, and she thought how odd that she'd gotten used to a gray cat accompanying their every move, one that didn't belong to either of them. Odder still that it felt right to be with Wolf, to be accompanying him on some errand for the sheriff.

Wolf was watching her, and she realized she'd fallen into a thoughtful silence. She tugged her seatbelt across. As it clicked into place, he started the truck.

"What's our mission?"

"To ask the key organizer to abort this event. Or at

least delay it."

Ugh. "We're going to talk to Dean Edmunds?"

He gave her a wry look and put the truck in drive. "Hardly. Though Grant would like everyone to think that about him."

"At the meeting earlier, he said he was head of the history department for the college, that the reenactment was under his leadership."

"Rita chairs the department and Grant implements what she decides regarding the program and this event."

"Rita?"

"The sheriff's sister. And my ex-wife."

"Um ..." She stopped, trying to decide how to respond before she said something dumb.

"Don't overthink it," Wolf said. "We've been divorced longer than we were married."

"Still."

He laid his arm across the console and opened his hand. She sat looking at it a moment, then placed her own in it.

"I won't say you'll like Rita, but I'm confident you won't dislike her."

She couldn't think of a single thing to say in response to that, so she didn't try. "Why would the sheriff send you to ask her instead of going himself? Do they not get along?"

"Because he thinks it needs to be said, and he knows she's going to refuse, which will make him mad. He doesn't want to deal with either her refusal or his anger."

"And you do?"

"No, but he was willing to bring me in on this investigation. Communication with Rita is a small price for that. Besides, he gets emotionally invested in their arguments. I don't."

She thought about that, about whether he was sending her a different, deeper message. Don't overthink it, she told herself, mimicking his suggestion.

She made herself relax and soon found herself enjoying the ride. The hillsides unfolded with the varying colors of spring. Wildflowers dotted the slopes in places. In others, the carpet of brown winter leaves remained. The sun was a larger-than-life orb of deep orange as it sank close to the horizon. Once or twice, she glanced back at Callahan who snoozed in the back seat. That seemed to be his usual response to a drive of any length.

Wolf's ex-wife lived far enough from town that the older homes in the quaint neighborhood were not right on top of one another. Kylah judged there to be several acres of well-maintained trees sprinkled across the manicured grass of her lawn. Wolf pulled into the drive and parked behind a low-slung sports car.

When he looked across at her, she lifted a brow. "And you're sure this was a good idea?"

"Seeing Rita is *never* a good idea, trust me."

She rolled her eyes. "Having me tag along," she said, although she was confident that he knew what she meant without the clarification.

"Trust me."

Biting back a smart-ass retort, she unbuckled her seatbelt then waited again for him to walk around and open her door. Though it wasn't what she was used to, a tiny part of her admitted it was nice. Just a tiny part, she told herself.

As she stepped down, Wolf glanced into the back seat. "Sorry, Callahan. Rita's not a cat person." Kylah was confident she wasn't imagining the look of affront in that yellow gaze. It surprised her to realize the level of her own curiosity, how interested she was to know what kind of person the woman Wolf had married and then divorced would prove to be.

From the affluent look of the house and neighborhood, it wouldn't have surprised her to see a servant open the front door, but that was not the case. The very pretty redhead welcomed them with a pleasant tone. Her smile was faint, almost non-existent, but neither did she look displeased at their appearance.

"You're lucky to find me home. I had a late meeting at the college, but I decided to cancel at the last minute."

Wolf introduced Kylah.

"I'm happy to meet you," Rita said. "Please do come in." She led them into a cozy sitting room opposite what appeared to be her office. Both rooms had wide doorways and at least one wall that was all windows.

Rita dispensed with pleasantries in short order, offering them tea, adding, "Or perhaps you'd rather a glass of wine?" which they declined. She gave Wolf a look that was direct and intelligent and, to Kylah's mind, amused. "I'm sure you're here to tell me about the latest incident because my brother declines to grow a pair and face me himself."

Rather than acerbic, her tone was droll and her hazel eyes were filled with wicked humor. Kylah liked her.

"I gather the grapevine is in excellent working order," Wolf commented.

Kylah noticed he was careful not to respond to the insult to her brother. She wondered if that was because he agreed with it.

The gleam of wit faded from Rita's eyes. "In fairness,

the conversation that was brought to me had less to do with the incident than about the scene Grant caused soon after."

Wolf's face reflected Kylah's own surprise. She couldn't imagine Grant making a scene, at least not one that would reach the ear of people who counted. And clearly Rita counted. Annoying someone else to that point, yes, displaying that behavior himself, not so much. A solid half-dozen questions came to Kylah's mind while Wolf waited for Rita to continue.

"It would seem the shooting, which may well have been random and accidental, rattled Grant so much that he demanded Audra," she glanced at Kylah, "his wife, not participate in the reenactment."

"And she refused," Wolf guessed.

"So, I gather. As vehemently as he insisted. Unfortunately, they were in a public setting."

"Has Grant, or anyone, suggested you cancel the event since we now have a murder followed by a second shooting?"

"Grant made some noises about it, but that hardly seems warranted. I'm sure Les will capture the person who killed that poor woman. I think the members of the historical society have the same confidence in our law enforcement that I do."

"Les is concerned, despite your confidence in him. And so am I." He paused before asking, "Why do you think the shots fired this morning might be random? Or accidental?"

Kylah found that odd as well, in light of the all too recent murder.

Rita crossed her legs and leaned back in the oversized chair she'd selected.

"Well, think about it. The murder appears to have been a very skilled shot to the heart. This morning's shots were off target."

"Not so far off." Kylah spoke for the first time. "The first went through the knapsack on my back."

Rita's eyes widened. "I'm so very sorry. I didn't realize you were there, that the shots came close to you. How frightening that must have been."

Her words made Kylah pause. The whole thing had happened with such speed. She'd been startled, reacting on instinct when she dropped to the ground in self-preservation. And her knees had been shaky afterward. But more than fear, she'd felt a flash of anger. Felt it still.

"It wasn't fun."

Turning her attention back to Wolf, Rita said, "As much as I love company, I do feel bad that Les sent you out here to tell me something I already knew. He forgets how fast bad news travels in academia."

Wolf cleared his throat. "That wasn't his primary reason for asking me to talk with you. With one murder and another attempt, which neither he nor I think was random, Les is concerned about being able to provide enough manpower to cover this event."

"You think Ms. West was a failed murder target?" Rita didn't wait for his answer but shifted her gaze to Kylah. "Do *you* think that?"

"Please, call me Kylah. And I don't know what to think. I'm not from around here. I've never been in a reenactment, and I don't know any of the people who are. I never met Maisy McGuire." She shrugged. "None of this makes sense."

She could feel Wolf's gaze on her face before he shifted

his attention back to his ex-wife. "Les wants you to shut down the event," Wolf told her bluntly. "And that's my advice as well. Before someone else dies."

Rita studied his expression a moment, as if she found it unexpectedly intriguing, then looked back at Kylah. "Will you pull out, go home, if I move forward?"

Kylah hadn't thought about that, but it didn't take her long. "No. I won't do that."

"What about others? What do you think they'll do?"

"I can't say. I have a contract and won't walk away from it. The reenactors have their enthusiasm for the event. It may well depend on whether they think the event itself triggered what has happened and will escalate from here. Or if the event is a good cover for a different plan."

She watched as Rita tapped her finger against her forehead as if the motion would help her think.

"Wolf, if we shut the event down, Les may never find the murderer. He may fade away to surface at another reenactment and kill again."

Kylah could tell by Wolf's expression he'd already thought of that.

He admitted as much, adding, "It's a concern, sure, but I have to think about this community first. I agree with Les. For once. There's no way even our combined teams can provide security across several hundred acres and thousands of participants and spectators."

Rita took a deep breath. "I'll consider the request, but we're just days away from the first scenario. Dozens upon dozens of participants have spent God knows how much money getting here, on hotels, restaurants. All significant boosts to the local and state economy and the prestige of our campus. Some of the audience have even made a week-long vacation before this first weekend. To turn them all away with no more than an apology and an expectation—or even a hope—they'll trust us when we advertise again next year, hoping they'll forgive and return? I don't know. I have to think this through."

Kylah sensed none of this was supposition for Rita. She was a woman who had done her homework and knew her facts, knew the impact to local businesses and what cancellation could mean for future plans for the event.

"How about an apology coupled with 'we don't want you to be a murder victim'?" Wolf suggested.

"Truly, I'll think about it," Rita said again. "And I'll talk with the other organizers, including the historical society members. That's the best I can tell you." There was a finality to her voice as she turned her attention from Wolf to Kylah. "You're going back to the fairgrounds? For the barbeque and dance this evening? The group we're bringing in is local but did have a country hit on the charts last year."

Kylah had forgotten the organizers within the college and historical society had planned a festive evening for the reenactors who cared to attend. She'd hoped to slip away before it got started, but it might be an opportunity to take a hard look at the people around her. Not everyone would be there, but would the guilty party be able to resist the urge to mingle and hear what was being said? And, after the scare she had this afternoon, she'd be damned if she'd give any appearance of hiding.

Chapter 12

Callahan greeted their return to the truck with a grumble, not quite a growl but definitely not a purr. Clearly, he thought they'd been with Rita longer than necessary.

"I'd hoped to have another evening alone with you," Wolf said as he pulled out of Rita's drive, "but I hear Rita's team went all out for this evening's entertainment."

When she didn't answer, he glanced her way.

She smiled at his expression. "Are you going to tell me not to overthink again?"

"Do I need to?" He sounded more curious than concerned.

She flashed him a quick, rueful smile. "No. Already working on that." And she was. It didn't come easy, although she could remember a time when it had. Before

Marty had ended his life and ripped hers apart.

"At least you can promise to dance with me. The band is as good as Rita said."

"I'll dance with you." She glanced down at her pants, still dusty from the arena, though she'd done her best to brush them off earlier. "After I shower and change."

"How about I drop you off at the hotel and pick you up when you're ready?"

There were a dozen reasons why that was not the best idea, why she should get her truck and be her own transportation, but all she said was, "Okay."

* * *

I watch, fascinated, as the crowd gathers; the reenactors arrive on foot, the academia in vehicles. All of them seem bent on having a good time. One woman has been murdered and another dodged—literally dodged—a bullet, yet the masses party on. Their enthusiasm for the evening seems a little inappropriate in light of recent events. I won't use the word unprofessional, but that would be close.

From my perch at the top of the stadium seating, I watch as the band plays and couples dance. I'm impressed at the speed with which a temporary flooring and platform for the band was set up in the center of the arena, but it serves its purpose well. The performers are versatile, offering an eclectic mix, everything from big band to pop rock to country. I don't prefer country but I'm intrigued by the skills of those able to dance to some of those quick-stepping tunes.

The crowd is equally varied. I note diamonds and rhinestones, denim with cowboy hats, pressed khaki and polos, a sprinkle of flirty dresses, and what I'm finding to be the inevitable Confederate gray and Union blue of authentic garb.

Even Wolf and Kylah have stayed more on than off the dance floor. Wolf's attention seems divided, half focused on the woman he swirls around in time to the music, half wary and watchful on the crowd around them.

My own scan of our surroundings is continual. Although I've seen nothing out of the ordinary, I still admit to prickles of concern. I can't ignore how easy it would be for a marksman hidden above to pick off someone on that dance floor, then slip through one of several exits that lead to the fairground proper. With the scattering of barns and outbuildings, there are far too many places to hide beyond those doors.

I'm not sorry when I see Wolf steer Kylah to the edge of the dance floor at last. From there, they walk toward the stairs that lead upward toward me and the concrete level behind me where tables have been loaded with all manner of nourishment. The seating around me has a good share of onlookers holding disposable plates loaded with food, cups containing some liquid placed at their feet.

I stand to stretch my stiff muscles as Wolf and Kylah walk past and fall in behind them, following to the food tables. I can see it's plain fare, but nothing to sneer at, and there's plenty of it. The servers aren't really attentive, but that's not a bad thing, as I'm used to taking care of myself.

While I wait for them to be even less attentive, I note a couple some distance away who don't seem happy with one another. I recognize the attractive brunette as Mrs. Edmunds from the meeting at the college. She seems to have snared the attention of Wolf's fishing pal, Logan. Whatever he's saying has drawn a frown. If I'm not mistaken, they're at the edge of disagreement, maybe even a full-blown argument. I wonder if I should draw Wolf's attention to this bit of drama, him being a keeper of the peace and all.

* * *

Wolf followed the cat's intense gaze across half the length of the building. Damn. He touched Kylah's arm.

"I'll be right back. Will you be okay for a minute?"

She glanced at him, a small crease of concern forming on her forehead at the change in his tone. "Of course."

He felt a flash that was equal parts irritation and amusement. Kylah was a woman more accustomed to taking care of herself and others than to having someone take care of her. The protectiveness he felt took him by surprise. Something to think about later, but—for now—he needed to head off a potential explosion. From the far end of the structure, Grant was bearing down on Logan and Audra, who looked less than happy with their discussion. And Grant's expression sure didn't give the appearance of a peacemaker as he strode their way.

Wolf reached them first, grateful for the small group of young people who momentarily blocked the aisle ahead of Audra's husband.

"Hey, Logan, you got a minute?"

Audra looked relieved. Logan flashed Wolf a look of pure frustration but the glare soon shifted to include self-disgust and regret as he realized he'd been making a spectacle of himself. And of Audra. He muttered an apology to her as he stepped back with Wolf.

Audra gave Wolf a quick glance, then moved away from them, blending with the crowd.

"Man, what the hell are you doing?"

"This whole thing needs to be shut down." Logan's voice was low and controlled, but not calm. More than frustrated, Wolf realized, Logan was angry, burning-up-inside angry.

"The reenactment." It wasn't a question.

Logan nodded. "A woman is dead. I hear Ms. West was shot at. Looks like any woman in costume is fair game. Grant could care less that Audra could get caught up in this."

"That's their business, man, not yours." One thing was for sure. The flame that had started in high school had never been extinguished. Not for Logan. Wolf had suspected, but this was beyond that suspicion, and he felt a stab of sympathy.

Logan met his gaze. He gave a curse and brushed past Wolf toward the row of doors. Wolf knew his sympathy wasn't appreciated, and he stared after Logan, knowing there wasn't a damned thing he could say to help.

"Your friend needs to keep his distance." It wasn't a friendly warning.

Wolf stifled a sigh and turned to face Grant. The man had made an effort to fit in with the crowd, but it didn't work for him. It never had. His khakis were too stiffly pressed as was his button-down shirt, but at least he'd forgone the tailored suits he preferred.

"He's concerned about the murder and the shots fired this morning."

"I can take care of my wife," Grant said.

"They're old friends. We all are. And we're all concerned about the reenactors." Wolf forced an easy tone he wasn't feeling. Logan's protectiveness for Audra was far more than that. That was more than clear to Wolf.

And apparently clear to her husband as well. "If he continues to harass us, I'll file charges."

Wolf frowned at him. "Continues? He's harassed you?"

"If he's your friend, you need to warn him away. It's ridiculous that he's still carrying a high school crush. It makes Audra uncomfortable."

Grant turned on his heel without giving Wolf a chance to respond.

It was just as well. There wasn't any way he could argue

with that. He'd seen Audra's discomfort for himself. He was going to have to talk with Logan, and his friend would be far from appreciative.

He made his way back to Kylah, and his heart lifted at the sight of her chatting with a group of women. He knew one of them, the others he didn't, but he had eyes only for Kylah. He wouldn't have minded seeing her in another dress, had even pictured how she might look, but the off-the-shoulders blouse with skinny jeans gave her a look that was pretty damn hot and had his pulse racing.

When she caught sight of him standing to one side, she extricated herself from the group and joined him. "Is everything alright?"

"With Logan? No, probably not. With me?" He held out his hand, and, when she took it, he expelled a breath, releasing some of the tension from the clashes with Logan and Grant. "Yeah. It is. Dance?"

They reached the dance floor, and he pulled her in close. He knew he could wind up sorry, sorrier than when he'd stood in front of a preacher and said *I do* to a girl he didn't love after her big brother, angry and unsmiling, had walked her down the aisle. Kylah lived on one side of the continent, he on the other. They had nothing in common, not background or lifestyle, not friends or family. But with her hand in his and her cheek nestled against his shoulder, he couldn't find it in him to be cautious.

* * *

Wolf spent the next morning at the sheriff's office with Les, combing through the autopsy report as well as the evidence the forensic team had gathered. Wolf had done enough research prior to their meeting to be certain they weren't dealing with some ongoing murder spree. There were no unsolved cases of death by antique firearm. At least not in this century.

Afterward, he gathered up all the notes he'd made and headed out to share them with Kylah and Jake. If Kylah had become a deliberate target, rather than a random victim because she was in uniform, she had a right to know as much as he could tell her without jeopardizing the investigation. Les had agreed, although with some reservations and reminders of what was at stake. Wolf hadn't needed any reminders.

Jake grilled burgers while Wolf propped against the side of the trailer and talked. The facts were simple. Maisy McGuire had been killed with one shot to the heart from a distance of twelve to fifteen feet. The Burnside rifle had been wiped clean of prints and left at the scene. The time of death was between six and eight that morning.

"I'd place it closer to seven or eight than six," Wolf speculated. "Better light then if you're planning to shoot someone." And would fit with Latimer's timeline of crossing those hills right before daylight, gave him time to complete the transaction before heading back to Fagan with the money from the sale.

Jake agreed, adding, "Not hard to be accurate at that range. But why in the hell did she stand there and watch while the killer lifted and aimed that rifle? No way he swung the barrel into position and made that shot cold. He'd have hit her easy, but dead center of the heart?" He shook his head. "Why didn't she drop and roll? Any damn thing to try to live."

"She had to have known him," Kylah said. "Had to

have trusted him."

"Or her," Jake reminded. "The killer could as easily have been a woman as a man."

"Both are true. Which is why Les suspected her partner," Wolf said. But Ella Necaise had a rock-solid alibi. Cameras don't lie.

"But if the person who shot Maisy McGuire was someone she knew and trusted, why shoot at me?" Kylah leaned back in one of the canvas chairs they'd unfolded. Callahan curled upon the one beside her.

"That's where everything gets murky," Wolf admitted. "It's possible that killing Maisy for personal reasons triggered something with the killer, sending them on a rampage targeting people who remind him of Maisy. Killing in cold blood isn't exactly the sign of a sound mind."

"There's no connection between me and Maisy."

"Other than the fact that you're both women. Both strong-willed. Both reenacting a Civil War battle," Jake retorted and flipped the burgers with expert care. The meat sizzled tantalizingly, and Wolf smiled at Callahan's immediate shift in attention from Kylah to the grill.

"You know Kylah so you'd know if she was strong-willed," and Wolf wasn't about to dispute that fact, "but what about Maisy? What makes you believe she was strong-willed?" He recalled Les saying the same thing.

Jake gave him a level look. "How many women you know would have stayed alone in that tent in the hills all night?"

Okay, he'd give Jake that, Wolf thought, but he'd have gone with brave there. Even so, yeah, strong-willed worked, too.

"What kind of reasons are those to kill a person?"

Kylah asked. "And who would know that both of us were strong women? Or even know for sure that I was a woman when those shots were fired at me. Those costumes were designed for men, and they aren't figure-enhancing."

Wolf could tell she was disturbed at the suggestion that the shots fired at her might have been intentionally aimed at her rather than at a figure in a Civil War costume, even a female figure in costume. He wasn't happy with the idea himself. He didn't bother to tell her there was no way a person who looked close enough wouldn't realize she was a female in men's clothing. The problem was, he didn't know how carefully the shooter had looked before picking a target. "We can't rule out that the target was the uniform."

A low growl from Callahan drew his gaze. The cat was staring at him and he sighed. "Callahan doesn't buy that theory."

Jake snorted his disbelief that the cat was communicating any such thought, and Callahan flattened his ears and glared.

* * *

Jake has bought himself some grace with his grilled ground beef, lean, just as I like it! Granted, I prefer steak to hamburger and fish to beef, but it's not bad for a noontime meal.

If I'm honest with myself, and I almost always am, I'm as perplexed by this case as the law seems to be. Like Wolf, my immediate thought is that Kylah's at risk but, the fact of the matter is, the next victim could be anyone. We don't have enough evidence to point in any direction. I admire the way Wolf kept on track with the information he shared with Kylah and Jake. He didn't give specifics of Latimer's comments, but he did give the two civilians as much as he could to help keep Kylah safe. The exchange also provided a chance for him to garner what insight she and Jake might have because they're enmeshed in the fabric of the re-enactment. As a deputized sheriff, he can only reveal so much and nothing that might jeopardize an on-going investigation.

* * *

Jake made himself scarce after lunch. He told Kylah he'd be at the barn and gave Wolf a considering look. Wolf watched him walk away, then turned back to find Kylah watching him.

"I don't like leaving you alone," he admitted. He knew that was what Jake had seen, what had the other man speculating.

"I've been alone a long time," Kylah reminded him.

Wolf knew he could take that any number of ways, but all he said was, "Not with someone shooting at you."

She smiled. "There is that."

He watched as her smile faded.

"I can't run away and hide. I won't do that."

"I know." They were standing close enough he could have reached out and pulled her against him. He didn't. Instead, he opened his arms to her. When she stepped closer, close enough that all he had to do was fold his arms around her, he closed his eyes and rested his chin against the crown of her head. She felt more right to him than anything had in a long time. "Just be watchful. Pay attention to what's going on around you."

"As much as I can." She drew back a little so that she could see his face. "My horses deserve and get every bit of my attention when I'm on them."

"Then I guess I'll have to trust Jake to watch your back."

"He'll do that. He always has."

And one day, he'd ask her about the man who'd had her back more than either of her parents or the man she'd married. And he'd thank that man for being there for her. Jake wasn't just an employee, he was part of her life, and Wolf was grateful for that.

For now, he had work to do.

* * *

Logan wasn't happy to see him. He didn't say it, but then he didn't need to. His expression spoke volumes. He even included Callahan in his unsmiling regard before returning his attention to the gun he had dismantled on the worktable in his shop. It was a small building with clapboard siding on the exterior and wide rough-cut boards for paneling inside. For all its innocuous appearance, Wolf happened to know it was pretty unassailable. The windows were high, long, and too narrow for a normal man to squeeze through. The pocket door behind the worktable led to a small room full of built-in safes to keep his clients' guns from the hands of thieves or the devastation of fire.

Wolf sat on one of the barstools and hooked the heels of his boots on the bottom rung. He watched as Logan worked in a silence that was anything but companionable.

At last, Logan spoke without looking up from his work. "I don't need a lecture."

"That's good, then, 'cause I'm fresh out."

When Logan finished cleaning the pieces and began reassembling the gun, he asked, "You want a beer?"

Wolf grunted. "Yep, but I'm on duty, so no."

That comment got Logan's full attention. His hands stilled. "You're here officially?"

"Nope, but still on duty." He hesitated. "You still of a mind that no one on the Boundary is behind what's going on?"

Logan gave him a piercing stare. "Why? Do you think different? You got something new?"

"We've got nothing at all, new or otherwise. That's the problem. We keep circling the mountain and coming up empty."

"Which means this is some crackpot who's not going to leave you a trail of logic to follow."

"So why are you so worried about Audra in particular?"

Logan put both hands on the table and leaned forward. "Because this *is* some crackpot who's not going to leave you a trail of logic to follow and because you and Les have zip to go on."

Wolf met him look for look. "But that doesn't answer the question 'why Audra'."

"She's a friend. An old friend and a good one. I care what happens to her. If this investigation doesn't come up with something soon, she'll be a target like every other female reenactor."

"That's assuming the target is always female."

"So far they have been," Logan reminded.

"True." Wolf got to his feet and said the one thing he'd come there to say. "Be on your guard with Grant, okay? He's not a front-and-center guy. He doesn't have the guts for it. You rile him about his wife, and he won't come swinging at you. He'll use his position and the law and a charge of harassment to get you arrested."

"And I'll post bail and then … nothing. I've spent a weekend in jail before for worse. So have you."

"We were kids with nothing to lose."

Logan looked around at the small gun shop that paid his bills. "Not much more now," was all he said.

Wolf sighed and let it go. Whatever was going on—if anything—was Logan's business.

But he disagreed with his friend on one point. There was a lot more Logan could lose if Grant decided to make trouble. His license to deal in firearms, for one. There was always a fine thread between the residents of the Boundary and those of the town. One that could easily snap. Both men knew it. Logan had decided to ignore the fact.

* * *

Kylah finished rubbing leather cleaner into the saddle and walked to the end of the barn where the hallway opened onto the road between the barn and arena. She leaned against the framework, enjoying the moment's relaxation. In the past few days, late spring had settled in with sunny skies and warmer weather and the woods beyond seemed greener by the hour.

It was that quiet time of day, moments before sunset. At some point, Callahan had returned without Wolf, strolling into the barn as if he owned it. Jake had headed into town for supplies about an hour earlier. Kylah had told him not to hurry. She'd take care of feeding and had plenty to read in the living quarters until he got back. She hoped he'd find a steak and a beer to enjoy.

As she watched, a young man—maybe a teen—strolled through the wide opening of the darkened arena then re-emerged moments later. If he was looking for someone, he didn't find them. He glanced toward the barn, but didn't seem to see her at its entrance. She tracked his loose-limbed walk toward the main road that led back into town. That was a long hike, but he was young. She could remember being that young, that filled with inexhaustible energy.

Vehicle traffic had slowed to a stop around the fairgrounds so she was a little surprised when a truck rolled past the youth, then pulled close to her own, and stopped with the motor idling. Taking her cue from Callahan who uncurled from his relaxed position beside her boots, she pushed her shoulder away from the barn post and waited. Her surprise deepened as Grant Edmunds stepped down from the truck and glanced around him, then walked her way. While she didn't share the irritation she could feel in waves from the cat, she didn't welcome a visit from the dean either. The fact that he had no idea how pompous he presented himself didn't make it any less unpleasant.

She nodded as he approached and was surprised to see that he looked tentative. Very unlike him. He was also dressed more casually than she'd seen him, almost carelessly, she thought.

He stopped and cleared his throat. "Ms. West ..."

"Kylah's fine. Really."

"Kylah, then," he said, starting over. "I wanted you to hear from me how sorry I am for the fright you received—the shots fired at you. I'd planned to tell you last night but found myself forced to deal with an unpleasant incident with Logan Yates. It's ridiculous that he still harbors a teenager's infatuation for my wife, one that was never reciprocated."

Kylah frowned, uncomfortable with his revelation.

None of that was her business. She was aware that some
people shared their personal lives with ease. She wasn't one
of them and didn't care to be on either side of that type
of exchange.

When Grant realized Kylah had nothing to say to his
comments, he tugged at a collar that didn't appear the least
bit tight and stumbled on. "But, of course, that's a minor
inconvenience, hardly worth mentioning in light of the
dangerous happenings of the past few days. I've advised
Sheriff Mitchell that I find all of this unacceptable."

Unacceptable? Murder? Now that sounded a bit more
like the pompous dean she'd come to know and to dislike.

"I'm not happy with it myself, but I'm fine."

"That's reassuring, and I'm relieved you didn't request
to be released from your contract although I suppose going
on with the show comes naturally to you."

"Runs in the family, you mean?"

He hesitated, perhaps trying to decide if she was being
sincere or sarcastic. She almost felt sorry for him. He cleared
his throat. "Yes, well, that and your own professionalism,
of course. You came to us highly recommended."

Kylah waited, not having a clue where he was headed.
She knew she wasn't helping him with his end of the
conversation, but even Callahan seemed to be losing
interest as he lifted a paw and began grooming himself.
And Callahan was one nosey cat.

Grant made a visible effort to regroup. "Rita is adamant
about going forward with the reenactment, even though
her brother disagrees with her." He looked troubled by
the history chair's decision, which surprised Kylah. She
thought Grant would be all about the bottom line—and
the glory—regardless of potential consequences. After

making all the appropriate noises of concern. "Of course, Les has never been able to rein her in, even when she was a teenager."

"I admit I did get the impression that would be her decision in the end." Kylah didn't comment on Rita's relationship with her brother, which was no more her business than Logan's feelings for Grant's wife.

Grant nodded. "She told me you and Wolf paid a call to discuss whether or not to move ahead with things." He looked around. "In fact, I thought I might find Wolf close by."

Ah, Kylah thought, enlightened. Grant's visit had never been about apologizing to her. He was hunting for Wolf but, for some reason only he understood, he didn't want to be obvious about it.

He cleared his throat. "I'm not at all certain the sheriff is up to being the lead on this investigation, especially considering the serious nature of the crime. Wolf has more specialized training. And connections."

"So, I've heard." No way was she commenting on his innuendo. Again, not her business.

"Well, I'm glad you're not rattled by these regrettable incidents."

Far less rattled than the woman who'd lost her life companion, she thought. She wondered if he'd apologized in person to Ella Necaise. She murmured another reassurance that she was fine and waited as he fumbled his way through a leave-taking that was long overdue.

Kylah watched, bemused, as the taillights of his truck faded into the gathering dusk.

* * *

Odd conversation, that. And I can tell from her expression that Kylah feels the same. I can't help but wonder if Grant is as inept an administrator as he is a communicator. One thing he did make clear is that he has no confidence in Sheriff Mitchell's ability to nail the villain.

Kylah and I continue to stand together, watching as the purples of dusk fade to the charcoals of night. I hear the distinctive motor sounds of Wolf's truck in the distance. As his headlights approach, glinting here and there through the trees, I realize this—Wolf's almost certain arrival—is why we haven't removed ourselves to more comfortable surrounds, like our cozy hotel room. And I wonder if Kylah realizes the truth of that.

Chapter 13

Sunlight sparkled on grass still wet with dew as Kylah rode Andy at a sedate walk along the wide path she and Jake had charted the previous day. It was something less than a mile in length and began and ended in sparse woodland patches. Near the center, where Albrecht Creek intersected the low hills, was one of the key battle scenes as laid out by the organizers. There no records of the actual battle fought along the tiny, winding creek but a significant number of artifacts had been found in this particular half acre. She and Andy would clear two easy jumps, the half-rotted trunk of a huge tree felled by lightning at some point in the past and the narrow creek itself.

Jake and Wolf followed on foot with plans to stop and

watch at the creek where she would take the second jump. For some reason, the thought of Wolf watching made her a tiny bit self-conscious. The realization surprised her as she rarely gave any thought to her audience, other than to ensure her mount had a safe space to perform, free from kids darting into her path. This was how she made her living, after all. An audience was another aspect of her work.

She shrugged the distraction of Wolf aside and focused her attention on the route she traveled. She reached the creek and nudged Andy over it at a slow jump rather than having him walk through. He needed to feel the bank on both sides, to know there was solid footing. She did the same when she reached the downed tree, enjoying the surge of muscles beneath her, the effortless lift over an obstacle created by nature. Their return trip would be at a much faster pace, not a full out run but at least a brisk canter in most places. The speed would help ensure their jumps were higher and more dramatic than they needed to be.

A few feet in front of Andy, a squirrel ran down a scrawny pine chattering. The horse held steady to his training but snorted in displeasure at the raucous sound. Kylah laughed, acknowledging an unexpected lift in spirits. The sun was shining brighter than it had in several days, the air smelled like nature, and she was astride a finished horse who enjoyed a good workout. Life felt good.

* * *

Wolf acknowledged the itch along his neck and put it aside. Kylah was a gifted horsewoman. True, her profession had its hazards, more than most, but she was knowledgeable, and she was skilled. Since meeting her, he'd done his homework, looked her up online, watched films of her work, the awards she'd won. She was viewed as an expert in her field. Wolf was good at research, and he'd dug deep. He should feel reassured, but the feeling lingered.

Jake didn't help things. Wolf kept his gaze focused ahead but he knew every time the other man glanced back over his shoulder or out to the side. He knew every time Jake rubbed the back of his neck the way Wolf wanted to do—but didn't.

"What's got you edgy?" he asked at last.

"Wish I knew," Jake admitted.

"You said you and Kylah walked this yesterday, picked the path she'd take, talked through the jumps."

"Yep."

Wolf glanced at the other man's tanned and weathered face but that was all Jake had to say. Wolf didn't press for an answer the man didn't have, but his own vigilance heightened. Though watchful, Callahan didn't seem to share their unease.

From time to time, the cat paused to examine the hoofprints pressed into the ground. There were clear imprints where the ground was soft but nothing the least alarming to be seen in their steady path. Though Wolf could detect that faint softening in the ground, it still felt safe and solid. Around them birds chirped and warbled and squirrels talked to one another in the tree tops, further evidence that Kylah had made an uneventful passage through.

"Creek's coming up ahead," Jake said at last. "That's

her second jump."

Wolf couldn't have said why the words heightened the faint sense of something wrong. Callahan picked up his pace, disappearing from view as he trotted over a small hilltop. Wolf heard the peaceful gurgle of rippling water, then the cat's piercing yowl.

Wolf's heart jerked as he and Jake broke into a run. Callahan appeared to be wrestling with something at the base of a tree a few feet from the open path they traveled. Jake uttered a curse, and Wolf knew the prickling on the back of his neck hadn't lied. He saved his breath as he raced ahead.

A thick rope had been stretched on their side of the creek bank, pulled tight and wrapped around stout tree trunks on either side. As Jake pulled his pocketknife, Wolf joined Callahan at the end of the rope. Grasping the heavy cotton, he put all of his muscle into pulling at the stake driven deep into the ground, the broad head buried in the decaying layer of leaves and dead grass. It inched up.

Wolf felt the jerk on the rope, then a loosening of the tension, as Jake's blade sawed through the rope. Jake's face was ashen as he looked at Wolf. "The log! Before she gets there!"

Without hesitation, Wolf took off in a dead run, not stopping to think or question or react. He had no idea where Kylah was on the path they'd traveled, if she were still walking to its beginning or galloping back toward him, toward a jump she might clear only to encounter a second obstacle she couldn't see.

Wolf had to hope the route she'd taken was as safe as what they'd traveled until now. He hadn't been with Kylah and Jake when they'd charted it, and he couldn't take the time to watch for the gelding's tracks in the ground ahead. His cell phone was useless because he'd seen Kylah hand hers off to Jake before she stepped her foot into the stirrup and swung her leg across the broad back of her horse, settling into the saddle with a look of coming home. Andy, she'd called him, stroking his broad neck in affection as he'd pranced in front of them.

A streak of gray passed him and Wolf didn't even try to deny the flash of relief that swept him. He trusted an animal's instinct every time and this cat seemed to have intuition in spades.

With sheer strength of will, he settled his frantic thoughts into action and kept running, grateful for the long afternoons of playing ball with a bunch of energetic teens. As he and the cat crossed the last low slope, the copse of woods Jake had described earlier loomed on the horizon. Wolf pushed himself faster. There, the fallen tree and, sickeningly, the same stretch of thick rope, white in the sun against the dark tones of lichen-covered bark. He couldn't be certain if he heard the thud of hooves or if the sound in his ears was his own heartbeat or Callahan's deepthroated rumbling of displeasure.

Without slowing to pull his knife, he scrambled atop the length of fallen tree and shouted her name. His voice echoed through the woods, and then he heard the rhythmic drum of hooves and knew horse and rider came forward at a brisk pace. He dug for his knife as he called her name again, sliding down to slash at the rope. The horse broke into the clearing, and Wolf shouted one last time as he flung the rope aside, praying it landed far enough or that Kylah saw and heard him before Andy's legs became entangled in the heavy cotton.

He stood in their path, throwing his hands in the air and willing the horse to see him in time. Kylah's eyes widened at the same moment the horse beneath swerved to one side, causing her to lose her seating. Wolf wanted to close his eyes, but he watched as she fought to stay in the saddle and calm the larger than average equine. Not until she was safe, did he heave a breath and let his shoulders drop.

"What the hell!" Kylah swung her leg over and slid down the gelding, hanging onto the reins until the horse quieted and quit pulling against her hold. "What's wrong? Where's Jake?"

Wolf still couldn't take in enough air to speak but he pulled her close, feeling her heart racing as fast as his.

"I could have run you over." Kylah's tone was bewildered.

"Least of my worries," Wolf said. He slid his hands down her arms, then stepped back and picked up the rope.

She stared in confusion as he pulled it into a coil in his hands. "What the hell?" she said again, more question than exclamation, now. "I just came through here, Wolf. No more than half an hour ago. I would have seen that."

"You would have," he agreed. His tone was grim. "Jake cut through the one at the creek and sent me running ahead."

Kylah looked sick and rubbed Andy's neck. "Jake would never have gotten here in time, not if it were just me and him today, not with his bad leg."

Wolf hadn't slowed long enough to consider why Jake hadn't forged ahead, but he knew Kylah was right. The other man wouldn't have made it although Wolf knew he would have died trying. He followed the rope to its end on one side and pulled up the wooden peg that held it to the ground. He studied it and the other piece of wood with two holes where the rope threaded through.

"That's a tensioner," Kylah said. "We were sent pictures and told we'd have to use similar to secure our tents if that's where we chose to stay. They didn't have to be real antiques but did have to be made in the same shape and from the same materials, whether wood or brass. I've seen them in use at Ella's tent and some others."

Wolf didn't speak as he walked to the opposite end of the log and pulled up the remaining set. He stood for a moment, staring at the objects in his hand while the image of her bleak eyes haunted him. He knew she was imagining her horse crumpled and hurting, while he was seeing her twisted and broken. Seething inside, he set everything down long enough to retrieve his phone and dial the sheriff's number. He got a recording and ended the call without leaving a message. Picking up the rope and pegs and tensioners, he moved back to Kylah. With his hands full he couldn't pull her into his arms but he stepped close and she leaned against him. "Let's go," he said gruffly, after a moment. He could've lost her today, and someone was going to pay for that.

Jake met them halfway. It took no more than a glance for Wolf to see that he carried the same type of rope and pegs as Wolf had gathered from the tree trunk.

"Sheriff's going to be waiting for us back at the trailer," Jake said, his gaze sweeping Kylah and the horse.

"We're fine, Jake." Kylah's tone was reassuring. "Wolf said your quick thinking sent him running. He made it to the tree and the trip rope before Andy and I did. Thank you."

Jake flicked Wolf a glance that held both relief and gratitude.

Wolf nodded at him. "And thanks for reaching the

sheriff. I tried him but didn't get an answer."

Jake reached for her reins, and Kylah let him take them. Wolf suspected she knew how much Jake needed to do something, anything, for her after the scare they'd had.

* * *

The sheriff waits for us, parked near Kylah's trailer with blue lights flashing. I'm thankful his siren is silent. My ears are more sensitive than most.

What a mess of a morning we've had, although it was not the disaster it very well could have been. I can all too easily see that horse thrashing upon the ground, Kylah pinned beneath his massive weight. I'm sure Wolf has been envisioning much the same. The sheriff hasn't yet exited his car and seems not to see us all trooping toward him.

Uh-oh, what's this? I see the profile of a half-grown human in the back seat. A young person already in trouble with the law? Kits have their troublesome moments, I concede, but not the angst found among human offspring.

As we reach the patrol car, the sheriff climbs out to meet us. I note he doesn't spare a backward glance for the young person in the rear of the car.

"What've you got?" *That's cutting to the chase as the humans like to say.*

Wolf drops the objects he carries into the sheriff's outstretched hand, but the rope remains coiled around one shoulder. "Booby traps. Two of them. Stretched behind two natural jumps along Kylah's practice route."

The sheriff scowls from Wolf to Kylah with a sidelong glance that includes Jake. He looks fierce, and I can tell he understands the risk this posed to horse and rider. "Who laid out the route?"

It's Kylah who answers. "The general route was laid out by the organizers, but Jake and I did a walk-through yesterday. We decided on a few twists and turns, some for effect and some to make sure Andy would have sure footing. We checked for holes and soft places, and we picked where I would jump."

There's silence as the sheriff ponders her words and studies the items in his hands. Finally, he says, "Looks like a kid's stunt to me and I may already have the culprit."

We all turn our attention to the back of the patrol car, and I hear Wolf say succinctly, "Aw, hell, Les. Rita needs to buy you a brain for your next birthday."

Ha! A zinger that was. I'll tuck it away for future use.

"Well, damn, Wolf. Show a little respect."

I hear the slightest edge of humor in the sheriff's voice. The stronger note, however, is sheer irritation.

"Earn it." *Wolf opens the back door and jerks his head at the boy inside.* "Climb out, son." *As the boy steps out beside him, Wolf asks,* "Have you done anything wrong, Case?"

"No, sir."

"Then straighten your shoulders."

Case glances at the sheriff then does as he's told.

"Why aren't you in school, boy? They give you a vacation day?" *The sheriff glares at him.*

"No, sir ... not exactly."

"Then what *exactly*? I can take you in for truancy if nothing else."

Case hunches his shoulders again, and I feel an immediate sympathy. The sheriff is a harsh one.

"It's test day. I'm exempt 'causa my grades."

"He's on the honor roll, Les." *Wolf's voice is quiet and proud.* "He worked his ass off for it."

The sheriff takes a deep breath, but some of the scowl eases across his face. "They don't give days off for that, Wolf."

Young Case likely sees a chance for reprieve, because he speaks up voluntarily for the first time. "My dad said I didn't have to go if I'd go clear the tree that fell across my grandpa's driveway two days ago. Took me a bit, but it's done."

"Your grandpa will vouch for you?"

Case nods at the sheriff's question. "Yes, sir. I promise."

"You live ten miles from the Boundary, Case. You walk all that way?" *Now it is Wolf's turn to look disbelieving, if only a little.*

"No, sir. My grandpa came and got me. I asked my dad to pick me up here. He comes right by here on his way home, so he said he would since it wasn't out of his way none."

"And why would you do that?" *Wolf sounds more curious than disbelieving. He's leaving distrust to the sheriff.*

Judging by the flash of trepidation on the boy's face that is a very good question and the reason holds importance for him.

"Mr. Jake said I could help him brush the horses sometimes, if my dad doesn't care."

I can see his answer surprises Kylah and Wolf as much as it does me. Jake scuffs a toe in the dirt but nods at the sheriff, affirming the boy's explanation.

"Were you in school day before yesterday?" *Hmmmm, I know where the sheriff is going with this one. That is the day that shots were fired at Kylah.*

Case nods.

"All day?" *The sheriff is pressing hard on the young man.*

Again, he nods.

"I can check that, you know."

"Yes, sir, I know. I was there."

So, even the sheriff must acknowledge it's back to square one on who set the trip-ropes for Kylah and her equine.

* * *

Wolf sent Case off with Jake to unsaddle and care for Andy. As much as Kylah wanted to do that herself, she wanted even more to hear whatever Wolf had to say to the sheriff. Underneath her bone-deep anger that someone could have crippled, even killed, her horse, she was worried that the someone would try again.

"It could still be some punk kid," the sheriff said testily.

"You were a punk kid once upon a time, Les, hard as that is for you to remember. How would you have put up a trip wire, whether it was a prank or a deliberate attempt to hurt someone?"

"Simple wrap and knot around a tree," the sheriff admitted.

"Exactly. I wouldn't have used this fancy set up and neither would you. Just a long piece of rope and a couple of knots."

Wolf turned his gaze on Kylah, and she knew where he was headed. She repeated for the sheriff what she'd told Wolf about the tensioners.

"Civil War replicas, huh?"

"The pegs may be replicas," she said in answer. "The tensioners may prove to be actual antiques."

Wolf studied the wear pattern on the items along with the sheriff. When he lifted his gaze back to Kylah, she knew he agreed with her.

The sheriff said at last, "I don't guess you were careful with fingerprints."

"Nope. Never gave it a thought. I was too damned busy trying to get it down and out of the way before Kylah came tearing through on that big horse."

She could have told Wolf that she was hardly tearing through the woods. She was always more careful of her horses than that. She let it pass for a host of reasons, not the least of which was the depth of emotion she heard in his voice. She wasn't used to anyone except Jake caring that much about what happened to her.

Wolf didn't pause long enough for the sheriff to respond. "There won't be any fingerprints but ours. Whoever drove those pegs as far as they could and pulled that rope as tight as they could will have worn gloves or wiped it clean when they finished, like they did the rifle that killed Maisy McGuire." He paused, as if to let that sink in, before adding, "We kept quiet our suspicion the revolver fired at Kylah was an antique so you can rule out a copycat troublemaker with this rope trick. We've got a real problem on our hands."

"We've had a problem since we found a woman with a hole through her heart," the sheriff answered.

"But I thought it possible that whoever fired that revolver at Kylah didn't know who they were shooting at ... may have targeted the uniform rather than the woman." Wolf reached over and tapped one of the tensioners that dangled from the coil of rope in the sheriff's hands. "This time they knew. Beyond a doubt, they knew. Which means this just got damned personal for me."

And Kylah felt the five-year-deep layer of ice around her heart start to melt.

Chapter 14

Kylah watched the intricate, white clouds drift across the late afternoon sky as Jake whittled at a chunk of wood he'd picked up somewhere during the day. He didn't whittle often, and when he was done, he'd hold something brilliant in his hand. And he'd be ready to say whatever it was he had on his mind. The cat dozed, curled in the chair beside her.

The absence of human sounds soothed her. She tried half-heartedly to identify the bird chirping in a nearby tree by its throaty warble but failed. She could no more focus on that than she could have arena work, which she and Jake agreed was best left until the next day. She knew he'd been as rattled as she was by the morning's near disaster.

She could, she supposed, have cleaned tack and been at

least a little productive, but it had felt good to do nothing other than sit here with Jake beside the trailer, if only for a little while. Slowly, her muscles had relaxed. From time to time, she checked Jake's progress as the intricate details of a miniature bayoneted rifle emerged beneath his hands.

Her eyes had drifted closed when his feet, which had been propped on an overturned bucket, hit the ground with a soft thump of booted heels. He brushed tiny curls of shaved wood from his jeans. Callahan grumbled at the disturbance.

She opened her eyes and turned her head to the side without lifting it from the back of her chair. "That's a beauty," she said of the work in his hand.

Jake gave a small hum she took for agreement. "Still needs polishing up a bit, but it ain't bad."

"You know you could make real money. That art store in Santa Fe said, *anytime*. They'll take anything you send."

"I'm savin' 'em for your kids."

She snorted. "That gets less likely every day."

"Going to be impossible if you get yourself killed. Maybe it's time we call this one quits."

She hesitated. Jake suggesting she walk away from a signed contract was a solid indication of how worried he was for her. She could forfeit the money without starving, but her reputation was a precious commodity. In this business, reputation meant as much as talent. With time, she could overcome any damage, but the thought of letting fear, Jake's or her own, drive her away didn't appeal to her.

She released the breath she'd been holding on a low, soft sigh. "I don't quit, Jake. You know that."

"What is it you're not wanting to quit on?"

He met her look for look, and she felt the challenge of his silence, heard the unspoken suggestion behind the question. "Wolf? Honestly … I don't know," she admitted. "After Marty, I thought, never again."

"And Wolf's got you thinking different." It wasn't a question.

"Maybe, but even if not, even if I'd never met Wolf, I wouldn't run from whatever is happening here. I'm angry, Jake, deep down angry. I want to see whoever tried to hurt Andy caught and punished. I'd stay for that if nothing else."

"They've come at you twice, now."

"Then I'll have to be more careful."

"Damn, Kylah." But that was all he said, and she knew the conversation was done. But she also knew how unhappy he was.

He stood and settled his hat more firmly. "That being the case, you need to call that movie company and have 'em overnight some more uniforms to you. Confederate or Union, either one."

She stared at him a moment. "Whatever for?"

"Wolf's boys—Case and his buddies—are going to stand watch when you make that ride."

"That's crazy! I know you didn't encourage that."

"Tried my damnedest to talk them out of it. I'm hoping Wolf will have better luck. He's playing basketball with 'em this afternoon. Case plans to tell him then."

* * *

"Hell, no."

Six boys in mismatched gym shorts and tee shirts stood watching Wolf, who glared at them. Case was their spokesperson.

"Wolf, listen, we gotta be there anyway. It's a class

assignment and an automatic test fail if we don't. We weren't gonna do the uniform thing, but it's extra points if we wear them and uniforms will help us blend in so that's kinda cool. Jake said he might could come up with some."

"Are you telling me the high school is going to turn out for this?" He hadn't heard anything of that.

"Not all of it. Just Professor Ingram's history classes."

"And not all at once," Adam, a tall and lanky redhead, chimed in as if to reassure.

"Seniors go first. We don't go until Sunday. Then the sophomores and freshmen after that. We get to pick where we stand, and I told Mr. Ingram last week we wanted to be by the cavalry charge because Mr. Jake said Ms. K.T. would be leading the way."

And how and when had Case and Jake become bosom buddies? He wanted a few answers there.

"You think I'm going to allow a bunch of teenagers to get mixed up in a murder investigation?"

Case looked at him with an expression between accusation and disappointment. "That ain't what I said, Wolf. We're not going looking for anything. We're going to be watching along where Ms. K.T.'s going to ride, making sure nobody messes with anything in her path." He paused, then added the killing blow. "I didn't have to tell you. We could've gone like we've been told we have to and you wouldn't never have known."

"Double negative, man." That came from Gray, who ignored the drop-dead look Case shot him. A muscular youth with a black hawk etched on his forearm, Gray didn't give the appearance of a scholar, but Wolf knew better. Wolf frowned at the hawk and hoped like hell he caught up with whoever was giving tattoos to teenagers on his watch, but that was another problem for another day. He solved them as he had time and that hadn't made the top of his list. Yet.

Right now, he had to man up with Case. "No, you didn't have to tell me, but I'm glad that you did and I apologize."

"So, you're good with this?"

Wolf knew he had to think hard and fast. Chances were he couldn't prevent them from being there but he'd do his best to keep them safe. "I'm good if the sheriff knows about the school assignment and if we put together a plan and I can count on you to follow it. I'll talk with Les tonight."

"What kind of plan?"

"The kind where you do nothing but watch and call me if you see anything. The kind where I know where each of you is, every minute. You all have cell phones, right?"

He got eye rolls on that one. It was a sad truth that too many of these kids came from families that might not be able to put a decent meal on the table, but every last member above the age of twelve—and some under—could send a text at a moment's notice.

"And you're all in agreement?" This time he got head nods in response. For now, that was as good as it was going to get. "All right," he said. "Let's break a sweat."

* * *

Kylah followed the gravel road around the outside of the arena, the gray cat close at her side. Callahan seemed as preoccupied as she felt. As much as she hoped Wolf could stop a bunch of teenagers from playing bodyguard, it wouldn't hurt to have some extra uniforms on hand for them. She'd rather have them overnighted here than the hotel. There was almost always someone in the office trailer that had been set up near the fairground entrance.

With afternoon light fading, it was possible the staff had all gone home although from time to time, she saw lights on and cars out front long past dark. But there was still daylight, though fading, and the walk felt good.

As she rounded the rear corner of the trailer, she recognized Grant's truck but not the late model, unpretentious little car beside it. The trailer door opened and a woman stepped out. Her attention was still focused inside so that she was half-turned with her back mostly to Kylah, but Kylah thought she recognized the dark hair as belonging to Grant's wife.

Kylah stopped at the sound of Grant's voice raised in frustration. "This is insane, Audra. You're being unreasonable, and I'd like for you to reconsider."

"It'll be fine, Grant. Really." The woman's tone sounded cool and unconcerned. If she was rattled by her husband's irritation, it didn't show. Kylah could admire that in a woman.

But she felt a wave of awkwardness at being witness to what appeared to be a small spat between husband and wife. If she could have backed away without being seen by either of the couple, she would have. She even took a step backward, but, as Audra turned to leave, the door opened wider, and Grant followed to the small porch, watching as his wife went down the steps. Callahan had settled onto his haunches at Kylah's feet, observing the goings-on with interest.

Without looking back at Grant, Audra got in her car and drove away.

Grant caught sight of Kylah as he turned to go back inside. His shoulders slumped, and she felt embarrassed for both of them.

"My apologies," Grant said with more dignity than she'd seen from the man yet.

No use in pretending she hadn't seen them or heard the exchange. She stepped forward. "And mine. I would have turned away if I'd had time. I'll come back tomorrow."

"No need for that." Grant straightened his shoulders. "I'm sure you need something or you wouldn't be here. Please. Come in."

Callahan looked up at her as if to say *may as well.*

They followed Grant inside. Kylah glanced at the whiteboard as she passed through the reception area. The board, which was a scenario layout depicting the upcoming events, looked busier than her first glimpse when she'd checked in with the staff upon arrival. She noted it caught Callahan's attention. He paused to stare at the squiggles and lines and initials of key reenactors, hers among them.

In one of the smaller back offices, Grant sat down behind a worn-looking desk. Kylah took the chair on the other side. "What can I do for you, Ms. West?"

"Kylah," she reminded.

He nodded.

"I'd like to have some additional costumes overnighted here if I could." She named the studio that would be shipping but didn't tell him why. Nor did she get the sense he was the least curious. No reason he should be. It wasn't his business, and she wished it wasn't hers, though she was caught up in it. Besides, she suspected his thoughts were still on his disagreement with his wife. All Kylah wanted to do was escape.

"That's not a problem, of course." He wrote the address on a note card and handed it to her. "I'll leave a note for the staff to be watching for it."

"Thanks." She got to her feet, hesitating when he cleared his throat.

"Ah … Kylah … you're a woman." Oh, no, no, no, she thought. Whatever he was going to say, she wished he wouldn't. Not with that opening. "And you've found yourself in a position of danger, for a second time now."

She sat back down. Okay … this might not be going where she feared.

At her expression, he added, "I was, of course, advised of this morning's incident." The pompous tone was back in his voice. "And I'm alarmed by the risk to all of the reenactors but—selfish of me, I suppose—I'm most concerned about the risk to my wife. Particularly, as it appears that it's women who are being targeted. I would prefer Audra not take part in the event."

Kylah blinked. What was she supposed to say to that? She certainly wasn't going to tell him she knew from her conversation with Rita that he and Audra had argued about this at least once already and in public.

"And, regrettable as it is, you, of course, heard her response to my worry. She intends to go through with her participation. Worse, she has some nonsensical notion of expanding her role, participating in another scene or two she finds of particular historical interest. It would make her visible and exposed for additional periods of time."

"I'm sure that's difficult for you to contemplate," Kylah offered.

"You have no idea. Worse," he hesitated, "she's pregnant. We've tried so long and had given up. I'm not concerned for her alone now. I'm concerned for our child." He pressed his lips together, looking exhausted. "I doubt we'd get a second chance."

Crap, she thought. "I'm sorry. Truly." It was all she could think to say.

"I thought, perhaps, you'd talk with her. Share how it felt to know you'd come so close to death or being maimed."

Part of her thought *what a jerk*. Another part of her understood his desperate request. "Dean Edmunds, I'll make a deal with you. If you get her to ask me how I felt about being shot at and having a booby-trap set for my horse, I'll tell her how it made me feel. But I'm going to be honest with her, so I need to be honest with you. I'm way more pissed off than I am scared off."

Looking startled, Grant leaned back in the chair that looked too flimsy for his size. "Well, I do understand you're a tough woman. You'd have to be in the business you're in. Show business of a sort, I suppose one could say. And traveling alone with your animals and … hired help."

And with that, he was back to being a full-blown asshole who irritated her instead of a concerned husband with whom she could sympathize. She managed not to roll her eyes.

Kylah got to her feet. "Yes," she agreed. "I am a tough woman. And I don't quit. You should be glad for that."

There was, Kylah thought, as she walked out, some petty measure of satisfaction in knowing she'd had the last word. That satisfaction, as well as the reminder of her own strength, had her feeling far less pensive as she and the gray cat strolled back to tell Jake she was heading out for the evening.

* * *

What a strange bird. Well, to be fair, many humans are, but this guy is more so than most. I understand the concern, however. It's instinctual in most species to want to protect their mates and their offspring from danger. Thank goodness, there's no risk of finding myself in that position. No such entanglements for me. I've got enough to keep me occupied, like the fact that Kylah has now been a target twice. Like Wolf, I don't believe it to be coincidental.

Which fact leaves me with two questions and the first is three-pronged. Was the failed bullet aimed at a uniform, a woman in uniform, or Kylah? Regardless of which, I have to believe the trip-rope was put into place to harm or even kill Kylah alone. Which brings me to my second question. Was the second incident, the trip-rope, out of frustration because the revolver shot missed or because Kylah was the target all along and the perpetrator wants to finish the job?

I'm also having difficulty meshing the skill of Maisy McGuire's murderer with the rather clumsy attempts toward Kylah. It is difficult to believe two individuals are at work but harder to believe that the expertise which felled Ms. McGuire has turned into something akin to a Keystone Cop comedy in the attempts against Kylah.

To top it off, I somehow need to share my concerns with Wolf man-to-man ... er ... cat-to-man. The difficulty is that feline to human communication is always a challenge. He tries his best to understand me, but he's no Dax.

Chapter 15

Trying to keep her mind focused on a shower and food, in that order, Kylah checked her phone as soon as the truck door closed behind her and the cat. There were two missed calls, one from her mother, the other number she didn't recognize. She hit play on voicemail. "Ms. West, Rita Stockton here. Please forgive me. I convinced Wolf to share your phone number. I'd like to talk with you at your earliest convenience."

A groan escaped her. Wolf's ex-wife was not necessarily someone she wanted to chat with. Regardless, she was one of the organizers. Even more, if she understood correctly, Rita Stockton was the energy behind the reenactment. She hit redial to return the call.

Rita answered at once and wasted no time asking to

meet with her. They agreed upon a restaurant in town in thirty minutes. Kylah ended the call and looked down at her dusty jeans and boots and shared a glance with Callahan. "What the hell," she said. If Wolf's ex wanted to see her spruced up, she should've given her more time.

* * *

Kylah pulled into a parking space and killed the engine before glancing over at Callahan. "Are you going to stay in the truck, come in, or scout out the surroundings?" For answer, the cat curled up in the passenger seat. Good enough, she thought. She lowered the windows. As cool as it was with the sun sinking on the horizon, she wouldn't risk the truck heating up in the last moments of daylight. Not with Callahan inside. No chance of rain and no chance of a thief taking advantage and stealing her truck. She'd hate to be the person who tried that with Callahan on board.

Before stepping out of the truck, she glanced at her phone. She'd heard two messages come in while she was driving. One from Wolf, suggesting he grill steaks for the two of them that evening. She liked the idea but wasn't sure she liked that she liked it and that didn't make sense even to her. About ten minutes after Wolf's message was one from Rita to let her know she'd decided to ask Wolf to join them and she hoped Kylah didn't mind, ending, Hopefully he hasn't already screwed up your friendship.

Kylah thought about that a long moment. Before she stopped herself, she answered Rita with, Is that what happened with your marriage? Second thoughts be damned, Rita was the one who had opened that door.

Rita's answer pinged back immediately. Mercy, no. I did

that with no help at all from Wolf, but I don't know what bad habits he's learned in the ten years since.

"Ten years," she said out loud. Callahan pricked his ears and met her stare. "That's a long time to be divorced." Or was it?

Sighing, she got out of the truck and went inside. The restaurant appeared to be a bit above average, both outside and in. She gave a second thought to her appearance, but there was nothing to be done about it now. A hostess escorted Kylah to the back of the restaurant where Rita sat alone in a booth. Kylah slipped in opposite her, keeping to the middle of the seat. She would rather Rita had chosen a table. She didn't want to wonder if Wolf would choose to slide in beside her or his ex, didn't want to think about what either choice might imply.

The other woman looked stylish in a cream-colored dress. "Thank you for coming on such short notice. Wolf should be here soon."

Kylah glanced up as a waiter approached.

When she ordered water with lemon, Rita asked, "Not a fan of wine?"

"Sometimes." She kept her answer noncommittal. She wanted a clear head until she knew what this meeting was about. Initially, she'd thought she might be going to receive a warning to stay away from Wolf, that Rita still called dibs on her ex-husband. But she couldn't see the sophisticated woman delivering that message in front of said ex. And after learning they'd divorced so many years ago? Definitely not.

Kylah saw Wolf before Rita did, perhaps because she'd been watching for him, and Rita hadn't. He stood at the hostess station as he scanned the room. As soon as he caught sight of Kylah, he moved without hesitation through the scattering of tables to her side of the booth.

"Hi," he said, sliding in beside her without asking. She moved to make room for him as he greeted Rita. The intentional brush of his thigh against her jeans was distracting, but she held her ground. Even when he gave her a faint grin.

Rita had been busy signaling the waiter back to their table. Wolf ordered a Malbec and *that* surprised Kylah. She'd seen him drink beer but not wine.

When the waiter left, Rita looked across at them. "I'll dive right in, shall I? Grant called me earlier." She focused on Kylah. "He said you were targeted again. I'm sorry. Again."

Kylah sighed. "It isn't anything for you, or Dean Edmunds, to apologize for."

"He did talk with you then?"

"Briefly." The Edmunds' small disagreement was no one's business but theirs, especially in light of the principal reason for Grant's concern. Rita may or may not know about Audra's pregnancy. If not, she wouldn't hear it from Kylah.

"He's concerned for the danger you were in, even more so considering how upset he found you afterward."

Kylah could feel Wolf's gaze on her. She felt a spurt of anger at Grant's misrepresenting her. "Actually, Rita, what I told Dean Edmunds is that I'm more pissed than scared. If that makes me seem upset, then, yes, I suppose I am."

Rita gave the faintest of chuckles. Understated reactions seemed her forte.

"What was the point of Grant's call, Rita?" Wolf was blunt. "To let you know what had happened?"

Rita shifted her attention to Wolf at his question. "He's less and less comfortable moving ahead with the reenactment. He suggested we postpone the entire event, perhaps to the fall, as midsummer is so hot and humid."

"What are your thoughts? Do you agree?"

"At this point, I'm not certain. I spoke with the historical society. That entire group is adamantly opposed to any shift in time. The fear is that we'll not only lose the momentum we have to this point—and it's been considerable—we may never regain it, even in subsequent years."

Wolf grunted. "And if someone else is murdered?"

Rita looked rueful. "Well, there is that possibility. And, human nature being what it is, that could push the outcome either way. Future participants and audiences will avoid us like the plague, or they'll come in droves out of morbid curiosity."

"You're not going to cancel, are you?" Despite wording it as a question, Wolf sounded certain of her decision.

"I'm not, no. I'll leave that decision up to the historical society. It's a great boon to our campus, and I think we were right to take on the bulk of the work, but it's their baby when all is said and done." Rita looked from Wolf to Kylah. "I can and will however, return your contract to you, if you like. No hard feelings. No questions."

"That won't be necessary." Kylah kept her tone quiet but very, very firm.

Rita nodded. "Good for you."

Wolf said nothing. Kylah had no doubt she'd find out later how he felt about her decision. But, in the final analysis, it didn't matter what either of them, what *any* of them thought. As she'd told Grant Edmunds, she didn't quit. If she were so inclined, she would've laid down and died five long years ago. Now, she was coming back to life, and she'd be damned if she'd let anyone take that from her.

When the waiter returned, Rita paid their tab over Wolf's protests and stood. "I'm late for a meeting, but I appreciate that you both took the time to talk with me. I hope there won't *be* any more incidents and all of this will go away."

"Optimistic, isn't she?" Kylah murmured as the other woman walked away on stilettos with more grace than Kylah had ever managed in boots.

"Nope. She's hardheaded."

Kylah smiled and cut him a sideways glance but decided silence was her best response.

Silence didn't save her as he added, "You should recognize that trait." He didn't wait for a response. "Did you see my message earlier?"

"Hmmm … I think I saw something about some guy grilling me a steak."

When Wolf got to his feet, she slid to the edge of the padded bench and took the hand he held out to her. He pulled her into his arms, and it felt good. It felt right. Maybe it wasn't time to stop thinking, but maybe it *was* time to stop overthinking. They dropped her truck off at the hotel where she and Callahan climbed in with him.

When she woke in his bed the next morning, it still felt good. And it still felt right.

Chapter 16

*A*s *much as I enjoy the sunshine, the warmth is unseasonable and uncomfortable. I watch as actors or reenactors or whatever they choose to call themselves tug at their collars. Kylah, however, looks as cool as the proverbial cucumber. Not that I'd know. I've sniffed one or two but not touched nor tasted and don't plan to. The scent isn't unpleasant but it isn't tempting either. I never bother with things that don't hit the right note with all three senses ... sight, smell, and taste.*

I didn't realize Jake would also be dressed out, as they call it. He cuts a pretty snazzy figure in military garments, something I wouldn't have expected, and looks as comfortable as Kylah wearing them. With one hand holding the reins of a sturdy looking buckskin, he keeps the other on Kylah's mount although that equine is well-trained and makes it obvious that he doesn't need steadying. In the din of confused actors trying to find their places, his eyes remain steady and his ears are forward with interest but not alarm.

But though Jake, Kylah, nor the horses are perturbed by the tumult around them, something pricks at my subconscious. Pricks hard. I've missed a clue or a warning but the harder my mental effort to grasp it, the more elusive it becomes.

That worrisome feeling is why I rounded up Dax. Fortunately, he fits right in. It seems that even the help who aren't part of the actual reenactment are required to be in uniform of some sort today. There isn't anything fancy attached to the one Dax is wearing ... no shiny buttons or such ... so I suppose he'd be considered a common soldier. The joke's on them, though. There's nothing common about Dax.

* * *

Wolf walked the route Kylah would take, from one end to the other. He stopped to talk with each of the boys who patrolled the course that had been laid out for her. He found them oddly, almost eerily, mature looking in their borrowed uniforms.

When he reached Case, the boy's shoulders straightened. It struck Wolf hard that, at sixteen, Case had already reached the age at which Civil War volunteers had been accepted. Some had been even younger. It struck him harder, still, that he was old enough to be Case's father. He couldn't fathom sending a son off in uniform.

He hesitated before speaking, but the drive to protect Kylah was stronger than the reasons for his hesitation. "Do you know Dusty McDaniel?"

"He's older than me, right? Lives on The Boundary?

"Right on both counts."

"I've seen him around. We don't run with the same crowd." That was all Case said, but his expression spoke volumes.

"He's a cousin." Wolf paused, the better to choose his words and his tone, keeping any hint of concern from either. "Let me know if you happen to see him around. I think he might be interested in today's activities."

He verified Case's cell phone was in his pocket, clapped the boy on the shoulder, and moved on.

A few yards further, red-headed Adam tugged self-consciously at the sleeves of his uniform, sleeves too short for arms that matched the rest of his gangly build.

"It's almost time, Wolf." The teen visibly struggled to contain his excitement.

Wolf smiled. "Almost." He wished like hell he could relax and enjoy the day as much as these kids.

"No one's going to lay a trap for Ms. K.T. Don't you worry."

"I'm not worried." But he lied. There would be another strike. It might not be here, and it might not be today, but with a woman dead and two attempts on Kylah, this wasn't going away. No matter how much Rita wished that it would. "You've got a good cell phone signal?"

"Yes, sir. I checked it."

Wolf walked on until he'd talked with each boy, reminding them again they were to do nothing except call if they saw anything worrisome. But he didn't trust them. Not for a minute. They were teenagers.

As he walked the last length, his glance met with that of Dax. Loose-limbed, deceptively relaxed, the man gave him a nod. Even if Wolf hadn't recognized the man, the cat draped over his shoulder was unmistakable. Wolf crossed the wide path to speak.

"Dax," he said in greeting.

They shook hands briefly. "I saw you talking to a few youngsters." Dax nodded his head back toward the way Wolf had come.

Wolf sighed. "Yeah. I wish they were a hundred miles away from here."

"Think they're ten foot tall and bullet proof, do they?"

"Pretty much. They're here to watch out for … things."

Dax nodded. "I expect that's why Callahan rounded me up. We'll be doing the same. I'll keep an eye out for them, as well."

"Appreciate it," Wolf said, then moved on the way he'd been headed. The exchange helped, but not a lot.

He made his way through a throng of Union uniforms until he reached Kylah. She was easy to spot, now sitting astride Andy who stood tall above the men around him. Too easy.

He put his hand on her knee, and she smiled down at him. Her smile faded at whatever she saw on his face. "Are the boys okay?"

"They're fine." He sighed. "You're a damned target sitting up on that giant."

Her expression softened. "Nothing's likely to happen in this crowd, Wolf."

He didn't agree. There was no safety in numbers. In the distance, he heard three soft, short blasts of a horn. He could feel the anticipation surge in the crowd around him, heard it in the ever-increasing hum of sound.

"That's our signal," she said.

"I'll be at the other end." But he didn't want to leave her.

He looked at Jake who met his gaze and nodded. "I'll be with her every step of the way."

But he could see the worry in the other man's eyes. Neither one of them felt good about this.

Wolf wanted to kiss her, but he only let his fingers tighten slightly on her uniform-clad knee, then he turned and strode away. He heard the drummer pick up the beat.

* * *

Kylah focused on the animal beneath her. He was as steady as she could have wanted. His training was faultless, she'd seen to that, but today held unknowns. The crowd lining the path at a respectful distance, the other horses following close behind, the beat of the drum all added an element of uncertainty. This was Andy's first such performance.

She patted his neck as they approached the huge, fallen tree. Giving Jake a cheeky grin, she pressed her knees to the horse's muscled sides.

Andy shifted to a trot, then a slow canter before she lifted the reins enough to signal him for the jump. He paid attention to nothing but the soft voice command, to her touch on the reins. She couldn't ask for better. They landed lightly but solidly on the other side, and he settled to a jog, then back to a walk when she asked it of him.

The second jump, the creek, was still some distance ahead, and she ran her hand down the length of his neck, murmuring her appreciation at what a good boy he was.

Jake moved in closer. "He's doing fine."

"Yes, he is." Kylah didn't *need* to hear Jake's compliment, but she appreciated it. Jake gave praise rarely and it meant something when he bothered. "He's a rock star."

Jake snorted at the term, and Kylah chuckled, glad that he seemed less anxious. "Have you seen Callahan?" she asked.

"I've spotted him a time or two, first on one side of us, then the other. He looks … focused."

Kylah thought that was as apt a description of the feline as any. Silly as it might seem to some, she liked the idea of the cat watching her back. She wasn't worried, although she supposed it would have been normal if she had been. Jake rode beside her. Six boys watched her progress like young hawks. And Wolf was at the other end waiting for her.

* * *

I've left Dax behind to keep an eye on the boys. My place is closer to the action to come.

The tingling along my spine has followed me through these sparse woods, and I still haven't pinpointed the root of it. Whatever I've missed nags at me. Andy took the first jump with perfection, but I'm still glad Kylah isn't cantering through the woods the way she did on her practice run. Earlier, I checked for holes that might've been dug then covered, pits designed to break a horse's leg and send his rider toppling, crushed beneath a mass of muscle and bone. I'm convinced there aren't any hidden hazards along the path. It's the human threat that unsettles me.

Immediately ahead is the creek that Andy will have to leap across. I pause in my tracks to watch, holding my breath until he's safely across and all four feet on solid ground. I see Kylah reach down to stroke his neck in praise. Yes, he's a good boy.

All that's left is the last little distance of this cavalry charge where there is to be another carefully orchestrated battle scene such as we watched yesterday. The choreography of the event had to have taken months. And there it is! Darn it! The memory that nags at me is the whiteboard on which every scene has been drawn. The whiteboard seen by every single participant as they sign up and pay the balance of their fee to take part in the fun. Our guilty party has means to know where each actor will be on a given day at a certain time, give or take minutes here and there.

If there's going to be an attempt on Kylah, it will likely happen when she reaches that destination and takes her place with the staged actors. I have to find Wolf fast and somehow warn him of the possibilities.

* * *

Wolf had begun to relax. One by one the boys were calling in and reporting that the cavalry procession had passed without incident. Ms. K.T. jumped the fallen tree. Ms. K.T. sure rode a nice horse. Ms. K.T. smiled at him as she went by. Ms. K.T. cleared the creek. Each one of their calls took a little more of the tension from his shoulders. Knowing when they were out of the line of action, so to speak, was as much relief as knowing that Kylah had passed safely by them.

The last message was text rather than a call. It came from Case and made him tense all over again. Dusty's here. Had a little conflict. He has a black eye. My bad. Not sorry. What the hell?

He turned to watch the slope, waiting for horse and rider to top the rise. The standard bearer came first, a sturdy lad in full uniform. There behind him, rode Kylah, unharmed, shoulders back, hair tucked under a cap but wisps escaping from the motion of her ride through the Carolina woods.

His respite was brief as he caught sight of the streak of gray racing toward him. The cat's agitation was indisputable. Callahan never expended unnecessary energy. Wolf turned, looking for the sheriff and any of his deputies. Les, vigilant, met his gaze and nodded. Searching the crowd of mingled audience and participants who awaited the arrival of the cavalry and the next scene to unfold, Wolf identified two deputies, out of uniform, but with intent faces that said they were on duty nonetheless.

Callahan reached his side and yowled. When Wolf bent to pick him up, the cat hissed at him and whirled in a circle, his face turned upward to the humans around him.

Wolf straightened and saw Kylah shifting her weight to dismount. Acting on instinct, he shouted, "Kylah, jump."

She hesitated, standing in one stirrup, her hand on the saddle horn, trying to find him in the crowd. He would be forever grateful that Jake didn't hesitate. The man kicked his leg free of the stirrup and flung himself toward Kylah, pulling her to the ground with him. In the same instant, he heard the sound of a shot fired, then another. As Wolf raced to close the distance between them, a woman screamed and a man shouted a hoarse curse.

Wolf dropped to his knees beside Kylah and pulled her into his arms. She looked around, dazed, as Jake grappled with two sets of reins, bracing his weight to keep the horses from bolting into the panicked crowd.

Les reached their side and bit off a curse. Seeing that Kylah was safe, he spun around in pursuit of whoever had fired the shots.

"She's shot," Wolf heard someone exclaim in a horror-filled voice. As he turned to offer reassurance, he realized the bystanders weren't looking at Kylah. They were staring at a point beyond. The two deputies he'd noted moments earlier pushed their way past the gathering and dropped to their knees.

As soon as Wolf loosened his hold on her, Kylah scrambled to her feet. "Stay here with Jake," he said. He didn't want her to see what lay beyond the small crowd. Dread filled him as he wondered if Rita had been there. He didn't recall seeing her.

Not Rita, he thought as he got closer. The crumpled figure, barely visible through the throng was a reenactor, he realized, catching a glimpse of Union blue. And a woman. Someone had removed her hat or it had tumbled free when she'd fallen. Dark hair. One of the deputies looked up as Wolf got close enough to recognize Audra's face. The deputy shook his head, his face expressionless as he spoke into his radio, calling for an ambulance. Beside him, a man in a Confederate uniform held a hand pressed to the wound at the base of her throat, but the blood seeped between his fingers. He looked as sick as Wolf felt.

He heard a soft gasp behind him and turned to press Kylah's face against his shoulder. He wasn't surprised she hadn't listened. She would never be a woman to stay in the background, not even for her own safety.

"Do you have Grant's number stored?"

She pulled back, eyes dry but reddened, face pale. Nodding, she pulled her phone free and handed it to Wolf. He found what he needed and shared the contact with himself. Then hit call.

"Hello." Grant answered the phone testily.

"Grant. This is Wolf. Where are you?"

"I'm leaving the office trailer at the fairgrounds on foot. Audra took my truck, and I guess she has her car keys with her as well. I need to get to my reenactment station."

"I'm headed in your direction now," Wolf lied, keeping an even tone. "I'll swing by and pick you up." With the phone still at his ear for Grant's response, he pulled Kylah close with his free arm and pressed his lips to her temple before signaling to Jake that he was leaving.

"Aw, hell, Wolf, you called me, didn't you?" Grant huffed the words. "I'm irritated at myself for being in this predicament, but that's no excuse for rudeness. What did you need?"

Grant sounded out of breath, and Wolf suspected the man hadn't walked anywhere in a long time. "We can talk when I get there." He hit end before Grant could ask any questions. This wasn't a conversation for the phone.

Jake moved closer to Kylah as Wolf turned to go. He didn't like leaving her. Not for a minute. But Jake would keep her safe.

Chapter 17

Wolf is running on emotion. He's in fear for his woman and not thinking with the clarity I bring to the table.

I watch as Kylah and Jake walk the horses back to the trailer, where I know they'll untack and load them for a return trip to the barn. I'll catch up with them there, later. For now, I have work to do.

As the crowd is dispersed under the calming guidance of local law enforcement, I study the trampled ground. There'll be little to no chance of a clear footprint to match the one in my mind, the one that was imprinted in front of Maisy McGuire's tent. Even if that were possible, there's nothing to say the shooter is wearing the same footwear, with the same tread.

However, if my calculations—crude but usually effective—are accurate, there might be a print or two at the base of a tree near where Kylah rode at the front of the procession of reenactors. It's worth a look-see. If Kylah was the target, as Wolf is convinced—and as I lean when the trip-ropes are considered—then today's shooter might well have been stationed above the crowd. When Jake pulled her to the ground, the barrel of the weapon would, logically to my mind, have been shifted downward to follow her path. If that's the case, then it wouldn't be likely that a bullet intended for Kylah would have hit another person, unless it was below the knee. The victim, Audra Edmunds, was notably tall.

It's also conceivable the perpetrator began firing wildly, hoping for a hit, as he saw his carefully laid plans on the verge of collapse.

I continue my musing as I circle first one tree, then another, but only those that wouldn't bend or sway beneath a human's weight. There aren't many. Most are young saplings. My guess is these slopes were thinned and replanted at some point.

The other possibility is that the culprit was at ground level, but would he—yeah, yeah, or she—have attempted a shot through a crowd of reenactors and audience with expectation of striking a particular target? If that's a yes, this person is skilled indeed and comfortable with their expertise as sharpshooter.

Then, again, there's always the potential that Kylah was not the target today, as I first thought, but only fair game as a reenactor or, more specifically, as a female reenactor. As Audra Edmunds would have been.

If I were a human, I'd probably give a big sigh at the many possibilities to be considered. But I'm a cat and way more tenacious than any human. Wolf and Sheriff Les will have every effort I can give to unearth the facts, unravel the threads of the mystery, and nail the bad guy.

And, at last, I see it, some distance away from the path. A booted print at the base of a stout tree with scratched bark, as if someone had scrambled up that trunk. But the tread isn't what I recall from the first murder scene. There's always the off chance that the person who climbed that tree had simply been looking for a better vantage point to view the pageantry.

Still, it's something to keep in mind.

* * *

Wolf called Les Mitchell as he drove. He was surprised when the sheriff answered with a bark. "Where the hell are you?"

"I'm on my way to Grant before some busybody or reporter gets to him."

"Damn." The sheriff sounded tired.

"I take it the chase was unsuccessful?"

"Hell, we didn't know what or who or where we were chasing. Those shots could have come from any direction."

So, yeah, Wolf surmised, unsuccessful.

"Hang on," Les said, "someone's calling in." A moment later he was back. "Wolf, I guess you better meet me at the morgue," he said heavily.

Wolf said a word he rarely used, then, "No, you tell those jackasses to keep her at the hospital, in a private room, in the emergency room, whatever. Wherever the hell she is, she stays until I get Grant there. I'm not taking the man to say goodbye to his wife in a damned morgue, Les."

"Yeah." The sheriff's voice was heavy. "Yeah, okay. I get it."

The sheriff ended the call, and Wolf was alone with his thoughts for another five minutes before he saw Grant striding down the long gravel road that led from the arena to the state highway. His Confederate jacket was slung over his shoulder and his face was red with exertion or temper or both.

Wolf slowed the truck and Grant stalked forward as it stopped. "What a mess," Grant started talking as he climbed in and pulled the seat belt across his lap. "I still can't get Audra on her phone."

Wolf put the truck in gear.

"She's not usually such a stickler for staying in character." The dean, still fiddling with his seatbelt, had yet to look at Wolf.

"Grant."

Something in Wolf's voice caught the other man's attention. "What?" Wolf couldn't speak past the knot in his throat, and Grant asked again, "What? What is it?"

"I'm taking you to Audra."

He glanced over. Grant was looking at him with the first hint of confusion. "Well, yes, she'll be there someplace, but we're assigned different areas. I can't say for sure where she'll be at this point."

"Audra's at the hospital."

* * *

Wolf left Grant at the hospital in a private chapel with his pastor and with family, his and Audra's. The drive to the hospital had been horrific, with Grant alternately sobbing and cursing.

The sheriff was waiting for him in the atrium. He shook his head as Wolf got close. "It's a hell of a thing."

Wolf didn't know what to say to that, so he said nothing.

"The doctors pulled a lead ball from the back of Audra's neck. It was wedged in the vertebrae. And one of my men picked up another linen cartridge a few yards from where she fell. Someone's leaving their calling card. We've got a damned serial killer on our hands, Wolf. I've called in the FBI."

Wolf would have done the same if he were in Les' shoes. "You've shut down the event." He didn't bother to make that a polite question. There could be no other option at this point.

"I've got every off-duty officer called in to move the spectators out, and I've told the unit commanders to have their teams sit tight. I don't want the reenactors scattering until I've determined who I need to talk with. And Rita needs a full report—in person—before I make it official with the damned reporters. Thank God she was at the starting point of the march this morning."

"Let me guess. You want me to head her way." Wolf said it without rancor.

Unexpectedly, the sheriff shook his head. "No, I think I need to go talk to her." He didn't seem to notice Wolf's brow lift in surprise. "She needs to hear from me everything that's happened, and what I'm doing about it. I'm meeting with a special agent named Jemson in the morning. I'll want you in on that." He hesitated. "If you're good with it. I know the Marshal Service isn't always crazy about mixing with the Bureau."

"I'm good with it." Wolf watched as the sheriff walked over and hit the elevator button to go back up. Maybe some things did change, after all. He watched as the doors opened, and Les stepped inside.

Wolf had one last thing left to do, and he didn't look forward to it. His thoughts were on Kylah as he walked out of the hospital. He'd call and check on her, but he had to see Logan before he could go to her.

* * *

The door to the gun shop stood open to the late afternoon breeze but a quick look proved Logan wasn't inside. Gun parts were scattered across the table where Logan usually worked. The unlocked door wasn't typical. He was careful about the property of the gun owners who trusted him, sometimes with prized heirlooms they wanted restored. Wolf left the shop and walked the path down to the creek behind the ranch-style house Logan had inherited when his parents died.

For a while Wolf thought it sad that Logan never married but, after his own divorce, he'd had a different opinion. Lately, he'd come back to thinking it sad. More so now than ever.

As Wolf cleared the trees, he saw Logan standing close to the water's edge, pole in hand. It was a peaceful looking scene with the breeze rustling the pines overhead.

Logan snapped the fishing line up, then flipped it back into the water savagely. His back was taut, and Wolf knew he'd heard. He sighed and spoke his friend's name.

The face Logan turned to him was dark with grief and with rage.

"Ah, hell, Logan. I'm sorry. I'm so damned sorry." It was all he knew to say.

"You find him, Wolf. You find the son of a bitch so I can kill him."

And, knowing what he felt now for Kylah, Wolf knew he'd have every bit as much rage inside. And the same desire to murder anyone who took her from him.

Wolf sat at the edge of the creek and waited until Logan finally sank to the ground beside him. They sat that way for a long while. Hearing the other man's shuddering breaths rip up through his chest slayed Wolf. He left only when Logan quieted and asked to be alone. "I'll be back," Wolf said quietly, "but call if you need me."

Logan wouldn't call. There was nothing that Wolf or anyone else could do for him now.

Wolf was at his truck, wanting only to get back to Kylah when he remembered the text from Case. He started the engine but left the truck in park as he called the teen.

"Hey, Wolf."

"Hey, yourself. Everything alright?"

"The guys are all a little shook up." Case, too, if his tone was any indicator. "Professor Edmonds … we heard she was dead."

Wolf sighed. "I'm afraid so."

"Sucks, man."

Without bothering to correct his language, Wolf agreed. "Yeah. What about you guys? Everyone okay?"

"Except Adam. Dusty kinda roughed him up so I kinda roughed Dusty up a little."

"Dusty's got a few years on you, Case, and a few pounds. That might not have been wise." Not to mention Dusty had a whole lot of mean on him.

"Nobody messes with Adam. Not his fault his uniform didn't fit too well. Dusty thinks he's a bad ass, but he ain't so bad."

As long as he wasn't toting a gun, Wolf thought. And the possibility was still in his mind, but nothing he could prove or question Dusty about. Yet.

"Stay out of his path."

"Planning on it."

But Wolf could hear the unspoken *as long as he stays out of mine.*

* * *

Kylah dropped her duffle bag inside Wolf's front door. She didn't necessarily agree that she'd be safer with him than at her hotel room. She did however accept that this was where she wanted to be. She wasn't sure how it had happened so quickly, nor was she happy that it had. But things were as they were.

Callahan certainly seemed content for them all to be in the same place at the same time. He made a leap for the center of the comfortable leather sofa where he curled into a ball. She suspected he was asleep before she had time to find her bearings.

Wolf flipped on some lights and hefted her duffle bag. "Damn, woman, what's in here?"

"Tee shirts, jeans, and boots." Her uniform.

She watched as he stepped into the short hall and the room she already knew to be his. She heard the soft thud of the duffle bag on the natural wood floor.

When Wolf emerged, he walked straight to her and pulled her into his arms. His hug felt like coming home. "Let's sit on the deck while Callahan naps. I've got some things to share with you."

As they passed through the kitchen, Wolf opened a drawer and a cabinet, coming away with the opener and a wine glass. He handed both to Kylah so he could grab beer and wine from the fridge. He held the back door open for her.

On the way from her hotel, she'd listened as he talked about Logan and Audra, their on-again, off-again romance through high school and college before she'd finally married Grant, who'd been in the drama club with her, always leading man to her leading lady. One of the many things, Wolf said, that ate at Logan throughout his own relationship with her. Jealousy, Kylah had thought, was an ugly thing. And a high school romance was never easy, even one strong enough to carry into college.

"They were crazy in love," Wolf had said finally, "emphasis on crazy. The last time they broke up, she took his boat to the middle of the lake and sank it." Kylah had a difficult time reconciling the dark-haired sophisticate with the passionate girl Wolf described. She supposed that gave her some insight into the scene between Logan and Audra at the reception.

The sky was deepening to purple as she sank into one of the rocking chairs that faced the woods behind Wolf's house. There was half an acre or so of yard between deck and woods, and Kylah caught her breath at the sight of fireflies dancing over the close-cut grass. "Oh, how beautiful!" She looked up to find Wolf staring down at her.

She took the glass of wine he offered and tucked a strand of hair behind one ear, self-conscious that she'd shown a little girl's pleasure at the sparks of flickering light.

"Yes," he said softly, still staring at her. "Beautiful." He took the chair beside hers. "I'm glad you're here."

"So am I," she admitted.

"And I'd be happy if that was all we had to talk about."

As much as she felt the same, she sensed he needed a sounding board, and not just about the death of a woman he'd known forever and the grief of the best friend who'd loved her just as long.

She waited while he stared out at the woods, occasionally taking a sip of his beer.

"I've been a lawman a long time. Les has been one

even longer. What's happening has all the earmarks of a serial killer. Les is convinced."

"You're not." It wasn't a question.

"I'm also not *not convinced*," he admitted. "Two women dead. Both reenactors. Both in uniform. Both killed by antique weapons. With no ties between them save those facts, it has all the earmarks of a serial killing."

"But?"

"It's the attempts on you. They almost fit the pattern but not quite. They were … clumsy … for lack of a better word. The revolver being fired at you. The trip ropes put up when you were on horseback."

"And if Audra was killed because the shooter missed me, that's clumsier yet."

"Exactly. Maisy McGuire was killed by a heart shot. Deadly accurate."

Nothing clumsy there, she thought. "So … two people, then, not one?"

"It's a thought I can't ignore." He hesitated. "But even that doesn't make sense. Les could find absolutely nothing in Maisy's past that would make her a target. But what about you? Have you ever been threatened by anyone? Had to deal with a stalker at any point? I know that's not uncommon in the entertainment business."

That was easy to answer. "Nothing like that. And, the thing is, most people never actually *see* stunt people. To the audience, the actors and actresses are *us* up there. Sure, most people know doubles are used, but during the action unfolding on the screen they never think of that, so we're not true *Hollywood*, not part of the star scene."

"I can see that." Wolf sounded relieved. "I had to ask. I have to know I can keep you safe."

"Without locking me in a closet?" she returned dryly.

"Something like that," he admitted.

Wolf stood and took her by the hand, pulling her to her feet. He took her wineglass and set it on a low table before wrapping his arms around her, tucking her tight against his chest. "Let's finish that wine later."

She laughed. "I need a shower."

"Good. I do, too. I'll wash your back, if you'll wash mine." And, with a quick kiss, he loosened his hold enough to take her hand and tug her back inside and down the hall.

* * *

Wolf woke to the warmth of Kylah's body against his, his phone ringing, and a gray cat staring him in the face. Without loosening his hold on Kylah, he reached across to the bedside table and grabbed his phone.

"Yeah."

"The special agent assigned to this case caught a flight this way, but he's in Oregon so it'll be late before he makes all the connecting flights. In the meantime, he asked for something I should have thought of myself."

Wolf glanced at his clock, wondering why his alarm hadn't gone off. Damn, Les Mitchell. Not nearly time, that's why. "What's that?" The sheriff didn't miss much but apparently the FBI thought he had.

"We need to know if any artifacts are missing," Les said.

Yep, Wolf agreed, that was a miss, for both of them. But not a huge one. Knowing what weapons were out there wasn't a clue to knowing who had them. He told the sheriff as much.

"And with the event shut down, I'm not sure how much it will help to know if something else *is* missing," Les agreed. "Not much window of opportunity now for a serial killer to make use of it."

Wolf couldn't argue with that. "Any lead is better than the one we haven't got."

Les grunted agreement. At least Wolf took it for agreement.

"Well, whether we get anything or not, it's something needs doing, and I've got an idea on how to go about it. I'm calling the two lead unit commanders and asking them to personally hold a weapons inspection first thing this morning. I'll accompany one. I need you to go with the other. Meet me at my office in half an hour." He broke the connection without waiting for Wolf's reply.

As he laid the phone aside, Wolf looked down at the woman in his arms. Leaving her before daylight was not how he planned to start this day.

* * *

Six hours later, Wolf looked around at the tents, still marveling at the amount of time and money these reenactors put into their passion for recreating the past. Both of the unit commanders had done exactly as asked, passing the sheriff's instructions to their officers to help carry out. Every reenactor had been cooperative in searching their belongings and verifying that every weapon they'd brought to the site was still safely in their possession.

After all weapons had been accounted for to the unit commander the sheriff had accompanied, Les joined Wolf.

The only thing missing for certain was a small-bore

revolver along with its container of homemade linen cartridges. If Wolf were placing a bet, he'd put money on it being the one aimed at Kylah as she'd walked through the woods and the same one that had killed Audra. The owner, an accountant from Maryland, had reported having six, of various makes and models, tucked away in several places in his tent. He emerged with four stating he feared two were missing. Rechecking, he located one, but—even after several sheriff's deputies joined in and took the interior of his tent completely apart—not the other. His face crumpled at the idea that one of his historic treasures had been used to take a woman's life. He didn't look afraid of being accused, clearly the thought never occurred to him that someone could think him capable of murder. When he was asked to accompany Les to the sheriff's department, all trace of color left his face. Wolf felt sorry for him but didn't bother to tell him it was protocol. He didn't think the guy was a murderer, but he'd learned to assume nothing, not where crime was involved.

Les took Wolf aside before he left. "I imagine all that will come of it is him filing a stolen property report."

Wolf agreed. "What next?"

"No one's missing any of those ... what did you call them ... tensioners? I've got a deputy checking out some online sites where Civil War stuff is sold to see if there were any recent purchases that stand out. And that agent—Jemson—won't get in town until close to midnight. Says he'll meet with us first thing in the morning. I'll see you then."

Wolf watched the sheriff walk away. Les looked old. He'd never thought of the man as old. Hell, he was getting old, too. And Audra's death had been hard on them all.

Chapter 18

*M*iles Jemson is the antithesis of movie theater characterizations of special agents. The man isn't charismatic in looks or manner. He's not hero material in the classic sense. Yet, behind thick-lensed glasses, his eyes hold the gleam of intelligence as he listens with quiet respect to first the sheriff, then our own Deputy Marshal.

Les and Wolf have worked in concert, but each brings a different perspective, having observed and been a part of different aspects as events have unfolded. On the table in front of Jemson are stacked several folders with reports and photographs. From the questions he asks now, it's clear to me, at least, that he studied them thoroughly and found the information they provide as inconsistent and confusing as we have.

Our surroundings are adequate at best. But that could just be me, as I'm no fan of metal folding chairs or cheap laminate flooring.

The location, however, is convenient. Now that the reenactment has been shut down, Sheriff Mitchell has taken over the office trailer previously occupied by the organizers. He and Wolf and Special Agent Jemson will use tiny offices in the back and this room in front for meetings of the mind. While the men brainstorm everything from the killing of Maisy McGuire, the attempts upon Kylah, and the shooting of Audra Edmunds, I turn my attention again and again to the whiteboard that covers most of one wall.

I did notice Jemson narrow a look at it as he walked in, but he didn't comment. I understand his lack of interest, as it's crudely drawn with many x's and lines, both solid, and dotted. The markings would make little sense to those with no knowledge of how the actual reenactments are orchestrated. From my observation, it's much like a movie scene and laid out in conjunction with the natural obstacles imposed by the geography of the setting. I can see all the connections, but, once again, something tugs at my subconscious, something I should identify and explore.

I focus hard on the squiggle I believe is the path of the cavalry that Kylah led across the low hills and, there, near the end I see it! A small notation. A slightly different slant to the handwriting. Despite the fact that I cannot read human writing, I know something is different. I think I should guide Wolf's attention to that spot. A movement catches my peripheral vision as Jemson stands, paper in hand and ...

Wait! No! Stop!

* * *

Wolf watched in amazement as Callahan, who'd been quiet and well-behaved until that moment, hissed and yowled, leaping toward Special Agent Jemson.

"What the—!" Jemson snatched his hand back, dropping the whiteboard eraser in the hasty movement.

"Get that damned cat out of here, Wolf," Les snarled.

Jemson was looking at the hand Callahan had swatted. Not a mark on it. He turned his attention to the cat who now sat staring hard at Wolf and shrugged. "I may have startled him."

"No." Wolf shook his head and said again, "No. He didn't want you to erase what's on that board. He sees something we've missed."

"Oh, for the love of Pete!" The sheriff all but rolled his eyes.

Wolf stared at the board for a long moment. It was damned hard to read with different colored markers used to depict different days. There was a legend at the top to help with that, but still. He looked at Callahan. "Show me."

"You're crazy," Les said. "You know that, don't you?"

Crazy or not, all three men were up on their feet by then, and Callahan leapt lightly to the chair closest to the whiteboard, the one Jemson had occupied. He turned to give Wolf a look, and Wolf slid the chair closer.

"Not just crazy," Les muttered. "Damn near certifiable."

Callahan lifted himself on his hind legs, bracing one paw against the bottom ledge of the board and lifting the other to touch a place Wolf easily identified by following the line from left to right. A line intersected by a crudely drawn creek and felled tree. There was a distinct 'kt' within a small circle at the beginning and at the end.

"Callahan's pointing out the end of the path the cavalry followed." With Kylah at the lead.

"That's not exactly earthshattering information. Everyone who was there knows where the route ended." And how it ended. The unspoken statement hung silently in the air.

So far Jemson hadn't commented.

"Hmmm." Wolf didn't stop his perusal of the markings on the board. "Callahan doesn't waste his time." Then he saw it. He placed a finger at one side of a tiny, uppercase A and looked at the cat. Callahan slowly lowered his paw, then his body, and sat regally on the chair. He closed his right eye in one slow, deliberate wink.

Wolf looked at Les. "Audra."

"But, so what? We already knew she was there and apparently that's right where she was assigned to be."

Jemson spoke unexpectedly. "The writing's different."

Les looked from the board to the agent, perplexed, but Wolf saw what Jemson had noted. "All of the other initials are in circles. This A isn't."

"The slant is different as well. Looks like most of the rest of the notations were made by a right-handed person. This one is left-handed."

Wolf looked at Les. "Audra was left-handed. We used to rag her about her handwriting in school."

"So?" Les repeated. "She penciled herself in. So what?"

"I don't think it matters she penciled herself in as much as it does that anyone coming in this office would know where she was going to be at the point in time she was killed."

"And?"

Wolf studied the drawing and thought back to his conversation with Kylah and the clumsiness he'd perceived in the attempts on her. "Makes it more likely you were right, after all, Les. I was beginning to doubt the serial killer aspect. This may indicate it was another expert shot like the one that killed Maisy McGuire rather than a clumsy attempt on Kylah that failed."

A rap on the door ended their conversation abruptly as all three turned to look as the door slowly opened. Grant stood on the narrow landing at the top of the metal steps—a Grant that Wolf didn't recognize. He looked ashen, defeated, a shrunken version of himself. The way Wolf would look if that bullet had hit Kylah.

"Grant." Les' voice was unnaturally soft and quiet.

Grant's eyes filled with tears. They glittered but didn't spill. "I ... Audra's purse. I think she must have left it here. It has things. Her things." Grant fell silent.

"Come on in," Wolf said. "I'll get it. Which office did she use?"

"The one all the way at the back. I wanted her to have the biggest one. Not be bothered with all the traffic up front those first few days."

As Wolf walked back and began opening desk drawers, he heard Les making introductions between Jemson and Grant. He found Audra's purse as Grant had suspected and started back down the hall, walking into the open area of the front where Jemson was asking about the whiteboard.

"Now isn't the time for questions," Jemson admitted. "But there won't be a good time. Not for this."

Grant shook his head heavily. "It doesn't matter. I have nothing to go home to now. What do you need?"

Jemson pointed to the mark Callahan had shown them. The small, uncircled A. "Can you tell me who wrote this?"

"Audra." Grant's voice was hoarse. "She wasn't supposed to take part all three days." He pointed to a place where the *a* was lowercase and circled like the others. "She marked herself in the two other days." He pointed to a couple more places. "We argued about it. Ms. West heard us."

"Why did you argue?" Jemson was still looking at the board.

Grant stared at the man's back, clearly incredulous at the question. "A woman had just been killed. Shot through the heart." He stopped for a moment. "I was afraid something would happen to her." He took a deep breath, then another. "And it did."

"That all the questions you got, Jemson?" Les sounded irritated.

"Yes. Of course." Jemson's tone was mild.

Les walked Grant out to his truck, and the special agent finally turned away from his study of the board. He met Wolf's look without flinching and expelled a sigh. "I always love my job," he said, "but sometimes I don't like it."

* * *

Wolf declined to go to lunch with Les and Jemson. He left his truck at the front of the office trailer and walked to Kylah's trailer. Jake had sent him a text earlier that he had the grill going. To his surprise, there were kabobs instead of hamburgers. Jake had gone to extra effort. He noted Callahan's appreciative sniff as the cat settled into one of the folding chairs. Wolf took one of the others.

Kylah came around the corner from the barn. The smile she gave him was sad. "How did it go this morning?"

"Interesting." He relayed Callahan's contribution and Grant's visit. "Grant said you walked up on their argument."

"Yes, and it was a very uncomfortable moment. I don't think Audra ever saw me, but Grant turned before I could find a way to make myself and Callahan disappear. He was more than upset."

"He said she'd added herself into more scenes." Wolf watched as Jake turned the kabobs as deftly as he flipped hamburgers.

"Yes, he thought she was taking unnecessary chances. For herself and the baby."

Wolf's gaze swung to her in surprise. "Baby?"

Kylah looked troubled. "I guess they hadn't told anyone yet. Apparently, she wasn't far along. Losing both must make it that much harder for him. He isn't the most likeable man I've ever met, but I can't help but pity him."

They were all three silent as they ate. Wolf thought the food was as good as any chef could have made it, but the events of the week weighed on him. He suspected it was the same with Kylah and Jake.

When they were done, he thanked Jake who headed into the barn, then pulled Kylah up from her chair for a quick kiss he would've liked to lengthen. But something was tugging at him. He ran a finger down one cheek, savoring the touch of her skin. He didn't want to leave her. "I'll be back, but it may be late. Stay close to Jake until you see me, okay?"

She looked at him quizzically. "I've got horses to exercise. I'll be here but … why?"

"Just a feeling. When I get done with Les and Jemson, I've got something I need to do. I'll explain when I get back." He laid his forehead against hers and closed his eyes. If anything happened to this woman, he'd be crazy for life. "There's still a murderer walking around, and I don't know who or where he is."

He waited until she disappeared into the barn with Jake before turning to look at Callahan. "Coming or going?"

The cat seemed to think about it for a moment, then

leaped down and followed Kylah's footsteps. At the edge of the barn, he glanced back over his shoulders as if to say *I've got this*. Somehow, that made Wolf feel a little better about leaving her. Not much, but at least a little.

* * *

It was later than he liked when he pulled away from the fairgrounds. He forced himself not to go looking for Kylah before he left. He'd make himself and her crazy with that. She'd been taking care of herself for years, and he didn't doubt she was a force to be reckoned with. And Jake was with her. And that darned cat, who seemed smarter than all of them put together. But cats didn't carry, concealed or otherwise, he reminded himself, and he wasn't sure Jake did either.

The sooner he got this done, he told himself, the sooner he'd be back. He needed to put some things to bed. That was all.

Logan was a six-pack in when Wolf walked around to his backyard. He'd knocked at the front door, but the lack of an answer didn't deter him. Logan's truck was there which meant Logan was there. The look on his best friend's face gutted him.

Wolf lowered himself to the grassy slope beside Logan, listened to the quiet of early evening around them, and wondered how to ask what he'd come to ask and say what he'd come to say. He didn't want to be here. But Logan had Wolf's back forever, and he'd done the same for Logan. He would now, too.

"I don't need a babysitter," Logan said without looking at him.

"That's not why I'm here." Wolf pulled a piece of grass and thought about how many times he and Logan had sat right here, the way they were now, talking about anything and nothing. Easier times. Happier times.

"And I'm not playing twenty questions with you."

"Not twenty. Just one." One damned important one. Wolf sighed. "Were you and Audra having an affair?"

"Go to hell." Logan's voice was filled with fury.

"Logan, I'm asking for a reason. Were you and Audra sleeping together?"

For a moment, Wolf thought Logan wouldn't answer.

"No." Wolf started to relax at the quiet word, but then Logan added, "There was never enough time with her. I wouldn't waste what little we had sleeping."

Wolf's heart sank. There it was then. And now he had to say what he didn't want to say. But he couldn't let Logan hear it from someone else. Worse, he couldn't let Logan hear it, unprepared, *in front* of anyone else.

"When Audra died, she was pregnant."

Logan lowered the bottle he'd been lifting to his lips and stilled. "Go away, Wolf. I love you, but I need you to go the hell away." His voice cracked. "Please."

Knowing how he'd feel about now, Wolf got to his feet and walked back to his truck. He had the door open, about to step in, when he heard Logan's howl of anguish. He put his forehead on the cold metal and felt his own heart split right down the middle.

Chapter 19

I'm headed to the shower," Jake said. "Why don't you come inside 'til I'm done?"

Kylah glanced at him. "It's too nice a night, Jake. I'll be fine. Besides Callahan's right here."

The cat blinked at her words.

Jake frowned. "Don't move."

Kylah stretched her legs in front of her. "I'm comfortable right here," she assured him.

The door shut behind him, and she sighed. The fairground was quiet at this end, and she was glad she'd fought Grant over their location. Just her and Jake and the horses. She glanced down at the comfortably curled gray cat.

Headlights aimed her way, and she felt her heart lift

when the truck pulled in at the office trailer. It could have been someone camping in the back, but only Wolf would have reason to stop at the trailer now that the investigation team had claimed it.

"Come on, Callahan. Let's go meet him."

The cat lifted his head at the sound of her voice and gave a complaining grumble. "Oh, come on, it's not that long a walk."

Still grumbling, the cat went with her the short distance down the gravel road to the small trailer. "Oh, that's Grant's truck, not Wolf's," she said aloud. A faint light glowed from behind the blinds of the front window. He was probably there to retrieve more of their belongings, his and Audra's. It seemed a sad thing for a man to have to do alone, and she stepped inside, Callahan right at her heels.

Grant stood in the dim hallway pulling an office door closed with one hand when she said his name. He stilled a moment, tightening his grip on the bundle in his other arm, before he turned to face her. "Ms. West. You startled me. I was gathering some things of … some personal things. I came this morning, but I had no idea that idiot sheriff had taken over the place. I'm not ready to be around anyone yet, so I left to come back when no one was here."

There was a musty smell to the place she'd not noticed before but that was probably lack of people. And that could explain the fine hairs that lifted along her neck. Or perhaps not.

Grant had begun to edge past her when something slipped from the stack of folders he carried. His free hand came up reflexively to retrieve it.

Kylah's heart lurched as her brain recognized what he held. A revolver, what appeared to be a true antique. Her gaze met Grant's, and her stomach sank. Her expression had given her away.

Callahan hissed, and she automatically shushed him. No point in the cat being shot as well.

"Pity." Grant was looking at her as if he felt anything but pity. "After I went to such great lengths *not* to kill you."

"But even greater lengths to kill your wife." Her lips felt so numb she wondered if she could even speak.

"She was going to leave me. I couldn't let that happen. Divorce is so sordid. We built our careers together. And other ... aspects ... made it even more shameful."

Pieces tumbled into place. "The baby."

"Not mine, of course." He grimaced. "And none of it the baby's fault. I actually thought about that after, as I hiked back to Audra's car. Wolf's call caught me midway. I had to think fast and turn in my tracks. Pretend I was walking toward the reenactment site. Wolf completely ruined the big moment I had planned, the drama of stepping out of Audra's car at the scene of her death. My devastation would have been dramatic."

"Quite the actor," she murmured.

"I took lessons from my dear wife who pretended to love me while screwing around with Wolf's best friend." He sighed. "And only Wolf got to witness my finest moment."

"But poor Maisy McGuire? What did she do to you?" She was stalling, of course, but she was curious as well. After all their conjecture about who and why regarding the death of Ella Necaise's companion, none of it would have produced Grant Edmunds as a suspect.

"Absolutely nothing. Nor did I do anything to her. But it proved convenient for me."

Convenient. The word chilled her. She knew she

needed time. Time to think and then act.

"Setting those trip wires for your little run through the woods, now that was damned inconvenient. As was climbing a tree and hiking through the woods and back in that damned uniform."

She breathed deep, trying to quell her quick rage at his words. Losing her temper would not help her find a way out of this. "Why did you try so hard to cancel the event when that would have ruined your plans?"

"Because it would be remembered that I *did* try. And because I knew no one would listen to me. They never do. Not really. Not that I tried hard, not with those that mattered."

"And I didn't." Still, he'd convinced her. She'd believed he truly wanted to put a halt to the event. Believed he was worried about the danger to his wife, to everyone. More fool she.

Her cell phone vibrated softly in the back pocket of her jeans. Jake, no doubt wondering where she was. He'd be concerned when she didn't answer, and she prayed he didn't come looking for her. Jake was tough but he was no match for a bullet.

"Not in that regard. You matter now. Unfortunately. You'll need to come with me, of course."

"Of course," she murmured dryly at his polite tone, thinking quickly and coming up with nothing. Nothing of value to use against Grant. Just an image of Wolf's face and fleeting glimpses of all they might have been. She wouldn't die without a fight, she thought, feeling unexpectedly savage even as she watched Grant with a wary gaze. She'd do everything she could to live, but ...

* * *

What a pickle. I hope Kylah stays as calm as she is now. I need time to think my way through this situation. For sure, I can't let this guy remove her from the premises. Jake may think to look for us here if he notes Grant's truck parked outside, but will he come in time and will he bring a gun?

I can't count on either. Kylah's best chance of escape is the moment we exit this trailer. The steps will provide a clear opportunity if she and I work together. I catch her attention and tilt my head toward the door, giving her a slow and deliberate wink. Without changing expressions, she returns that wink with equal slow deliberation. She understands me, but I don't dare get cocky because Grant won't dare allow her to live. Her life is at stake, and the responsibility of saving her is on me.

I give a sigh of relief as I hear a truck, and—yes—it's Wolf's this time. If Kylah had my good hearing and my primal, instinctive memory, she would've known it wasn't Wolf before we started down the path. But, likely, she would've come anyway. Her heart is very large.

I'll have to trust my knowledge of Wolf's nature … that he'll note the truck that really shouldn't be here and stop rather than drive on past. Even if he isn't suspicious but, like Kylah, if he steps in to check on Grant, it gives me more of an advantage than I have at the moment. I can manage, if forced to it, but I'd be happier with better odds.

Now, hopefully, I can make enough of a racket to keep Grant from detecting the sound of Wolf's truck approaching. That lamp atop the file cabinet is a good candidate for the task. I ease my way forward, snaring the cord with one paw and begin to pull. Slowly, stealthily. I can only hope my movement doesn't trigger an unexpected response from Grant. No pun intended.

What a satisfying crash. And—most fortuitous—as I think it came just as I heard the soft thump of a truck door closing. What with Kylah's obliging shriek, timed perfectly as she tracked my cunning movements with her wise gaze, plus Grant's somewhat bland cursing, even the tread of boots on the steps is muffled. I feel it against the pads of my paws rather than through my sensitive ears. I add a plaintive yowl to the mix for good measure.

Hopefully, Kylah's deliberate yelp alerted Wolf sufficiently that he's forewarned and armed. I can tell by the way she watches me that Kylah, as much as Grant, remains unaware of Wolf's presence.

But, oh dear, there's a noise at the back door as well. Is it friend or foe?

* * *

Jake had stopped feet from the door of the trailer at the look on Wolf's face. Wolf knew he'd also heard the crash and Kylah's cry from inside the trailer. Jake's expression was grim.

Wolf pointed to himself then toward the side of the trailer, even as he motioned Jake up the front steps. Wolf needed a diversion to get to Kylah. He prayed Jake would understand and keep a clear head and steady nerves as he walked toward the front door while Wolf circled around to the back.

He'd heard Callahan's yowl and the sound was reassuring. Kylah was far from alone. Desperate as Grant might be, Wolf could only hope he wasn't suicidal.

Wolf had learned to pick locks in high school. Not one of his stellar attributes, but he put it to good use now. He had no idea how much time he had, but realized his time had run out as he slipped stealthily through the back door.

Callahan, silent and unmoving, stared at him then turned his attention back to Kylah and Grant who faced the front entrance.

"Open that door real slow," Grant said. "Then you're going to go down the steps even slower. I advise you don't take your mind off this pistol."

Once that door was open, Jake would be exposed but Wolf didn't dare rush Grant from the rear. Not with a gun pointed at Kylah's back.

The door swung out, and Wolf's heart jumped painfully in his chest. But the front steps were empty. Kylah stepped through, immediately curling herself into a ball, throwing herself sideways away from the steps. Callahan hissed as the front door slammed shut in Grant's face.

In the next moment, Callahan was clawing his way up Grant's pants leg howling like a banshee. Grant's finger pulled the trigger reflexively. As that shot went wild, Wolf spun him with one hand and chopped the pistol from his hand with the other.

Drawing his fist back, Wolf made it count … for Audra, for Logan, for the baby … and for the ten years Grant had shortened from Wolf's life with the sight of a gun trained on Kylah.

* * *

Jake isn't accepting any kudos despite the fact that he was wise enough to position himself atop the porch rail on the hinge side of the door. He knew he'd be hidden behind the door as it swung open. His miscalculation was in expecting Grant to step out first to make sure no one was watching. With his intent being to knock Grant cold by slamming the door on him, Jake barely missed hitting Kylah instead.

The possibility still has him rattled.

Now that Grant has been shoved into the back of a patrol car, securely in deputy custody and on his way to the county jail, we've all squeezed into the office space once more. There's no room here for anyone to be comfortable, but it's conveniently at hand.

Jemson's shoes crunch on the broken lamp base as he moves to stand near the file cabinet. He looks pained at the sound, probably anticipating there will be some damage done to the leather soles of that expensive footwear he sports.

The sheriff hasn't quit scowling, and Wolf hasn't turned loose of Kylah.

* * *

Wolf savored the feel of Kylah tucked safely against his side. He'd never get over the ice-cold fear of a pistol aimed at her back by a man who'd already killed without compunction or compassion. A small bruise bloomed on her cheek, and every time his glance fell on it, rage toward Grant Edmunds swept through him. He suspected there were worse marks elsewhere from her acrobatic tumble out the front door.

"Grant sure had me fooled. Murder." The sheriff shook his head. "Huh. I'd never have thought the man would have the nerve to pull a trigger much less the skill to play his part that well."

"Maisy McGuire's death is what doesn't fit in with the rest of this." Wolf had grasped quickly enough that the attempts on Kylah had been a decoy in Grant's plan to kill his wife. The fact that Kylah could easily have been hurt or even killed had apparently been of little consequence to the man.

The sheriff looked dubious. "I think Grant has proven himself cold-blooded enough to put a bullet through an innocent woman's heart to divert suspicion from himself."

"I won't argue with you there, but I have a hard time believing he came up with something that complicated." But he could be selling the man short. Again.

"I'm not ruling out Grant, not yet, but I may have to take another look at Ella Necaise," Les agreed reluctantly. "The security camera at the rest stop cleared her of actually pulling the trigger, but there may be something I've missed. Some motive."

"You're talking murder for hire?" Jemson looked interested at the notion.

"Or even another three-ring circus like this one."

"Regardless, I'm confident we can rule out a serial killer."

Wolf thought the agent's tone held a touch of disappointment and asked, "Even though all of the weapons used were Civil War relics?" He agreed with Jemson, but that was another aspect that bothered him. Another aspect that didn't fit.

Les looked thoughtful. "Grant might have been using artifacts as a statement of some sort."

"He might," Jemson conceded. "Then again, this wouldn't be the first instance of a copy-cat killer latching onto something for convenience."

"Convenience? Like just happen to be lying around?"

"No, more of a useful camouflage which would suit Mr. Edmunds' purposes. I suggest the first thing you do is determine if he has an alibi for the morning Ms. McGuire was murdered."

Kylah, who'd been silent through their discussion to

that point, said, "I think you'll find he does." They all turned to look at her. "He admitted to murdering his wife and her unborn child. All but admitted he intended to kill me. I didn't plan to make it easy for him, but that was his intent. But he denied killing Maisy. Said her death was convenient."

"Which falls in with Jemson's thoughts," Wolf said. "But Ella Necaise doesn't push that button for me."

* * *

As these humans ponder the same ground over and over in their conversation, I do the same with the mental images stored from the first murder scene. The rifle placed upon the crudely constructed table. Footprints that simply turn away and disappear into the tree line. Something about these pieces still don't fit that puzzle for me, either.

I somehow have to persuade Wolf to let me study those photos he took. Oh, for a human with a cat's understanding. But that doesn't happen very often.

First, the cell phone. He placed it on the table after calling his immediate superior once the not-so-good dean was carted away. Carted away is a satisfying phrase. Brings to mind a movie Dax and I once watched of jailers in jolly old England transporting prisoners in open-sided carts along cobbled roads while decent citizens pelted them with animal droppings and rotted vegetables. We should do that in America.

But, back to the phone and photographs.

I bat the device to Wolf, and he glances at me questioningly. When he doesn't pick up the phone, I nudge it a little closer. I'm careful, as I don't want it to slide off the edge and hit the floor.

I give Wolf an appreciative rumble deep in my throat when he picks it up.

"He wants you to call someone?" *Kylah asks.*

Oh, no, no, no. Surely, now that the conversation has turned to the unsolved murder of Maisy McGuire, Wolf has to be thinking along the same lines as I am. The scene. The investigators report. His photographs. We've missed something and he knows it as well as I do.

And, yes! After another moment of thought, he taps an image on his phone and photos light his screen. Perfect! Technology. You gotta love this stuff. The last pictures he took are of the murder scene. Lucky for us, he's not one of those people who take photos of every tree and sunset that catches the eye.

Wolf scrolls through each slowly, allowing me to take my time studying them. The series ends with the panoramic scan of footprints and there it is, the damning evidence I failed to identify earlier. I can only hope Wolf's quick mind captures it as well.

"Les."

"Yeah?"

"I think we need to talk with Mr. Latimer again."

Wolf is a smart human indeed.

Chapter 20

The next morning, Wolf headed into the woods with a pair of binoculars slung around his neck and a thermos filled with coffee in his backpack. He had some thinking to do. He'd never considered leaving these hills, never wanted to, but he was considering it now. And that startled him as much as his feelings for Kylah, which were too strong, too soon, but more real than anything he'd felt in his life.

He knew he was going to ask her to stay, to see where they could take this thing they'd started. What he didn't know was what he'd say if she countered by asking him to go with her. He'd never lived anywhere else. Never wanted to. He knew every inch of the Qualla Boundary and the land around it.

He hiked to Albrecht Creek and gazed at the slopes around him. Other than trampled grass, there was little remnant of the interrupted reenactment. This part of his home stomping grounds wasn't the prettiest, but he'd spent hours here as a boy. He and Logan.

He couldn't think of the boys they'd been without thinking of the men they'd become. Looking back, he could see that Logan had never given himself a chance with any woman after Audra. He'd dated here and there and some had been lengthy relationships, but Wolf couldn't ever recall Logan looking at one of them with the longing and heat his gaze had always held for Audra.

And, that, Wolf realized, was where he was with Kylah. These hills, Logan's home, his friends had never healed Logan's heartbreak over losing the one woman he could love. Wolf knew they'd never be enough to heal his heart if he let Kylah walk away without him.

Taking a deep breath, he let his gaze trace the rolling terrain in front of him with slow appreciation, then he turned around and headed for home and the questioning Les had set up with Raymond Latimer.

* * *

When Latimer walked into the sheriff's office, he didn't seem nearly as nervous this time as last. Nor was he dressed in Civil War clothing. Instead, he wore khakis that appeared clean, but could have used ironing, and a plaid button-down shirt with the sleeves rolled to the elbow.

"We appreciate you coming back to talk with us," Wolf said. He waved him toward a chair on the opposite side of the desk. Les sat in a chair and rocked it back against the wall.

"I don't mind, if it will help wrap things up. Most of us need to get back to our homes."

"It's a shame that won't happen for Maisy McGuire."

"Heard y'all caught the killer."

"News travels as fast here as anywhere," Les nodded. "And about as accurate."

Latimer looked uncertain, as if he heard the hidden meaning. The man wasn't stupid. He might or might not be guilty, but he wasn't stupid.

"We do have someone in custody for the death of Audra Edmunds," Les allowed.

Latimer stayed quiet, but Wolf noted a slight frown now creased his forehead.

"You said Maisy McGuire was stirring something in a pot when you reached her camp," Wolf reminded him. "Are you sure she wasn't already seated? Already eating?"

He could feel Latimer's mind racing, trying to decide what answer to give. And why he'd been asked. Wolf didn't let him stew over it for long.

"You see, Raymond, Ms. McGuire had already started eating when she was shot through the heart. The autopsy gave us that. Whoever murdered her carried the rifle when they walked out of the woods. They stopped in front of her table and shot her. Then they walked up, laid the rifle on the table and walked at an angle back the way they'd come. Your footprints gave us that." Callahan had given *him* that.

The lawmen watched as Raymond Latimer absorbed the words, as his face crumpled. "It wasn't murder, I swear to God, I never meant her harm. Shouldn't have been no bullet in that rifle. Commander Fagan always uses blanks. Only wanted to scare her. She was such a bitch about the rifle, couldn't I see she was infantry and didn't I know Burnsides were issued to cavalry only. Made me out to be stupid." He stopped, then said again, "I wanted to scare her. Take that smug look off her face."

"I guess you accomplished what you wanted then," Les said flatly. "The look on her face as she lay soaked in her own blood wasn't smug at all."

* * *

Les had only a few more points to clear up after that. Latimer answered without hesitation, never calling for an attorney although Les reminded him more than once of his rights. As he was led from the room, Wolf looked at Les and sighed. "So, Fagan sent the wrong rifle with Latimer, and a woman dies."

"That was mistake one," Les agreed. "Mistake two was Latimer not knowing what was in that carbine."

"Even Fagan said he only used blanks," Wolf reminded.

"He may have. I did a little reading on that particular rifle once forensics confirmed it as the murder weapon. It has a documented flaw as far back as the war. An odd-shaped cartridge that occasionally got stuck in the breech after firing. Fagan may well have loaded a blank—behind a live cartridge he didn't know was there."

"So, Latimer may not be charged with murder."

Les nodded, looking grim. "Depends on how forensics on the rifle plays out. I'm glad the rest of this is on the DA to sort through, but I'll tell you it would've been better if Latimer had called for help."

There was that, Wolf thought. He picked up his hat to go. "I suppose we could toss in a couple more mistakes.

Maisy McGuire had a choice in how she reacted to Latimer bringing the Burnside rather than the gun she was expecting. And Latimer had a choice in how he reacted to her harping."

Les nodded. "They both chose wrong."

* * *

There was one last conversation Wolf needed to have about the particulars of the morning Maisy McGuire was murdered. He found Case dribbling the basketball on the sidewalk outside of the gym where he waited for Wolf and the others who habitually played after school.

The boy looked up with a quick smile, a lock of too-long hair falling across his forehead. He brushed it aside with quick movement. "What's up, Wolf?"

Wolf returned the smile. He liked this kid, liked that he didn't quit, liked that he looked after his siblings. "We solved a murder today."

"That's cool, then." Something in Wolf's expression must have caught Case's attention. He gave the ball one last bounce then secured it under his arm and added, "Right?"

"That's cool," Wolf assured, "but I'm left with a question."

Case didn't tense, but he did look suddenly cautious. "Sir?"

"The morning you found Maisy McGuire in the woods, you were hiding something or flat out lying to Sheriff Mitchell. Which was it and why?" He used his no-nonsense voice, but there was no harshness in it.

Wolf watched as Case fought the look of belligerence that had once been his go-to with every adult. But not with

Wolf, not anymore. Case won, and the look faded but his shoulders dropped. "I told the sheriff I was alone when I found her. I wasn't. Cash was with me."

Wolf took a deep breath. Case's kid brother. What the hell …

"We were hungry. Daddy said he didn't have money for food so we took his rifle and went squirrel hunting. Cash is a better shot than me. He got a couple squirrels and missed a couple. I was afraid one of those missed shots hit that woman. I sent Cash home with the squirrels and the gun. I wasn't going to let him get caught up in the system." Every single one of the kids Wolf worked with knew what that meant.

"I'd never let that happen, Case." But Wolf couldn't blame the kid. Case had come a long way in the trust department, further even than some of the others, but the man fate had decreed he call a father kept sending Case back a step. Wolf hated knowing that. "You've been worrying ever since, haven't you?"

"Yes, sir."

"You don't have to worry anymore. It's over, Case. No one's going to be looking at you or Cash for anything to do with her death. I promise."

Case slowly nodded. "Okay."

"Now, how about we get a little practice time in before the others show up. And, don't be bouncing that ball on the sidewalk. It's not good for it."

Case grinned. "Yes, sir." This time he spoke those two words in a very different tone.

* * *

Wolf didn't reach the fairgrounds until nearly dusk. Jake stood in his usual spot at the side entrance of the arena, watching as Kylah put one of the horses through his paces. Although the event wouldn't take place, Wolf had learned enough to know how important it was to hold to their exercise hours and that just riding circles around the arena was boring for them. Light maneuvers both entertained and kept them sharp.

Wolf leaned against a post on the opposite side of the opening and studied Jake across the short distance that separated them. "You saved her life."

"We all did," Jake said.

"If you hadn't been smart enough to position yourself where you did, if you hadn't reacted as you did, slamming the door in Grant's face and separating her from the gun aimed at her back ..." Wolf's words faded as a chill traced down his spine.

"That might be so, but it put you in greater danger."

"Not something I care about." Wolf hesitated not knowing how to go about what he wanted to say. And ask. "You've been with her a long time."

"A while." Jake was looking at him more closely now. Wolf sensed the shift in intensity in Jake's scrutiny.

"I'm going to ask her to stay. I honestly have no idea what she'll say. But I do know how much she depends on you. How much you mean to her. I don't think she'd want to be here without you."

At his words, Jake turned his gaze back to Kylah and her horse. For a moment, Wolf thought he wasn't going to get a response. And he'd be left wondering.

"Rodeo taught me that life is a bitch. You're ridin' high, and a fall brings you to rock bottom. Rodeo also taught me that home is where you make it. I make mine wherever K.T. goes."

The silence after that was lengthy, then Jake spoke again. "That boy—Case—seems to me he'd be a good hand with a horse. Asked if I thought he could learn to ride. I expect I could help with that."

Wolf nodded, and his heart eased. "I expect you could." If Kylah agreed to stay.

* * *

Kylah was content. Spring had turned indecisive, and the air held a winter chill, but the night was pretty and clear. Jake had brought out the propane heater for warmth and served hamburgers complete with buns, lettuce, tomatoes, and anything else they could think to put on them.

She and Wolf sat close but not touching. Their canvas folding chairs, with Jake's, were arranged in a semi-circle, the better to hear Wolf's depiction of the meeting with Raymond Latimer and how Callahan had led him there. The fourth chair stayed empty as the cat had chosen her lap. She suspected that decision was in response to the unexpected cold more than any need to be near a human.

"So, Callahan turned the tide, again," Kylah murmured, and the cat rumbled a purr against her ribs.

"I like to think I would've eventually figured it out." Wolf chuckled as the cat's gaze swung his way, "But I suspect Callahan knows better."

"I guess he and Dax will be moving on now that the event is over." Kylah felt more than a little sad at the thought. She'd grown fond of his sassy self. She'd never considered owning a cat before—or allowing one to own her—with her nomadic lifestyle, but she was giving it some real thought now. Callahan seemed to adapt to his surroundings without difficulty. So, maybe.

"What do you think, Callahan?" Wolf asked. "Think your guy might want to look for more work around here and settle in for a while?"

Jake got to his feet. "Y'all carry on with that conversation. I'm going to feed."

Kylah smiled as he walked away. "He's as much in awe of Callahan as we are. Not that he's going to admit to it."

She had no doubt that Dax and Callahan would be leaving soon and so would she. She'd already begun to accept that saying goodbye to Wolf wouldn't be easy, but the wrench she felt as that moment drew closer was so much more than *not easy*. Apparently, she wasn't a love 'em and leave 'em kind of gal, she thought with a forced flippancy that soon faded. The truth was, she'd never expected to feel this way. Not again.

She watched as Wolf got to his feet. "Take a walk?"

"Sure." She stood and took the hand he held out to her.

Callahan declined to follow, settling into the warmth of the chair Wolf had vacated.

They walked slowly, ambled really, hand in hand with no particular destination.

Neither spoke for several minutes, but Kylah wasn't one to wait for the inevitable. She'd always found it better to meet facts head on. "I guess the sheriff is going to let us all disband now."

"Pretty much. He'll want contact information to be able to reach out to key witnesses, of course."

"Of course," she murmured.

The silence between them was so complete she could hear the crunch of gravel beneath their feet louder than the beat of her own heart.

"I'm hoping he won't have to worry about that where you're concerned."

Kylah stumbled over an invisible rock. "As in, not need to talk to me?"

"No." Wolf stopped and tugged the hand he held. When she stopped as well, he turned her to face him. "As in, what if you stay? What if you're close enough he can stop by and chat with you if he needs to."

"I'm not good at guessing games," she said hesitantly. Her heart was in her throat or, horrible thought, still wildly beating in her chest but completely visible to him.

"You don't need to be. Not with me. I'll never make you guess." He studied her face, as if trying to read her. Or memorize her. "Stay with me, Kylah. Please."

A thousand thoughts and fears and questions filled her mind, clamoring to be heard. In the end she pushed all of that aside for one reason. In her chaotic mixture of emotions, the one thing she didn't feel was doubt. "Yes," she said softly.

Wolf pulled her close and murmured, "Thank God."

"So … what do we do now?"

"Nothing hard about that," he said, and then he kissed her.

* * *

Kylah seems in a pensive mood, which I find surprising given the happy ever after exchange last evening. I sure hope second thoughts aren't popping up now that it's time for me to leave.

I note Jake's small frown as he drinks his morning coffee and watches as Kylah's grows cold in her hand. He senses her brooding as well. "What's on your mind?"

Kylah pulls a folded slip of paper from her pocket. "This." *She unfolds it and begins to read.* "I guess if you're reading this, I did it. Finally. I'm sorry, babe, I can't carry the weight inside me anymore. Love you most, M." *Her voice breaks on that last letter. I've overheard enough conversations to know the M stands for Marty, the husband who was not strong enough for this life.*

Jake says nothing. Just watches and waits.

"I feel guilty letting go. There's no one left to remember Marty. To care that he lived and that he died."

"Letting go doesn't mean forgetting, K.T. You'll always care, and you'll never forget. I believe Marty loved you enough to want you to be happy. I think Wolf is the guy to make sure you are."

Kylah looks across at Jake and there are tears in her eyes, but they don't fall. She takes a deep breath. "I think so, too, Jake."

"At least I won't have to worry about some stranger picking you up drunk in a bar anymore."

"Well, those two got me home safe, now, didn't they?" *A faint smile curves her lips as Jake snorts and gets to his feet.*

Kylah stands as well, and I leap from my perch on the steps of the living quarters. I might as well watch the fun of cleaning stalls and saddling horses until Dax is ready to head out. There will be exciting times to come as Wolf helps Kylah and Jake relocate these and her remaining horses to his neck of the woods, as they say. But me and Dax ... we'll be someplace down the road by then.

We match Jake's unhurried pace toward the barn, and tiny scraps of shredded paper drift from Kylah's fingers to land in the dust at my paws.

Kylah's heart has moved on at last, and I believe that to be a good thing.

A Note from the Author

In May of 2017 Chris Janson co-wrote "Take a Drunk Girl Home" and released it on his album *Everybody* that September. That December it was released as a single. In June of 2018, I posted the following on FB.

That moment! Driving home, thinking about anything and nothing, and listening to a country station. A song catches your attention and, just like that, a scene slides into your mind and you 'see' the beginning of your next story. You don't know who she is and you don't know her story but you know it's there in your mind, waiting to be written. That's the kind of moment a writer loves.

"Take a Drunk Girl Home" was the inspiration for the opening scene of this story.

* * *

Thank you for taking the time to read *Callahan In Action*. If you enjoyed it, please consider telling your friends or posting a short review. Word of mouth is an author's best friend and is much appreciated.

Thank you!

Susan

Susan Yawn Tanner is a bestselling author in the romance and mystery genres. When she isn't writing, she's either tending her horses or barrel racing. Although she lives less than an hour from the Gulf of Mexico, the white sandy beaches of Mississippi can't compete with the lure of arena dirt.

Scan the QR code to sign up for Susan's newsletter where she announces new books and exciting giveaways.

susanytanner.com